Only requiring a simple word or phrase to fire her imagination into a story, June's pleasure is to run with a theme and produce a complete story, no matter how random the starting point. It is a skill and a challenge - and this book is the result. Within these pages, June has encapsulated her wandering thoughts, producing characters that reveal themselves through rich internal monologues and fine illustrative detail. Her stories drift between different ages, cultures and viewpoints with ease, extracted from a lifetime of observation and contemplation - and of course there is a smattering of autobiography in the mix too - nothing is sacred. So beware all who enter - you may already be in here...

A Collection of Short Stories

by

June Kashita

ISBN 978-1-7395589-1-8

Exmoor News
exmoornews.co.uk

Also by June Kashita
This Was My Africa, Living With Changes
and
The Willows

For Ceri and Simon

and

with grateful thanks to Sarah Gibb

Contents

A BLANK PAGE

I look at the blank page.

This is the moment I feel the anticipation. This is the whole new beginning and who knows where it may lead? The blank page has different things depending on my mood; it may be concealing a hidden secret bursting to be released and my fingers will barely be fast enough to keep pace. Conversely, it may be lying dormant, unwilling to be prised from its comfortable niche.

How can I know what lies there, waiting for me? If I have my own ideas, it can fight back as I formulate them, can reject, muddle and confuse until I lose direction. But if I let the blank page open up and receive me … then we can go hand in hand – but I must trust, trust the destination is known. Ultimately, we will arrive.

The not knowing is part of the excitement. I'm embarking on a journey when I have no idea of its length or destination. It will all unfold as we go, blank page and I. Partners in a mysterious process that I do not understand.

I wonder occasionally, how was it for the monk in his cell copying in such laborious detail the verses in his holy book? The parchment would not be consistently smooth to receive his scratchy quill. And again, the inks and the paints he had ground and mixed so carefully may not have been reliably consistent. And as he patiently inscribed each letter, adorned each capital – was he ever seized by the desire to break free and write words which hitherto existed only in his mind? Share a message with us, something new and fresh? Or are the strange creatures peering from the G or H his sole outlet for his creativity? The curl and flourish on some letters, a sign of a momentary desire to share something new? I like to think so. Think that as he blew on his chilled fingers one frosty morning, that he paused and smiled in satisfaction at the gryphon or the extended y as its tail entwined the space nearby.

All a far cry from this blank page as my fingers hesitate above the keyboard. Each time I fear this moment and then the anticipation reminds me that the journey is about to begin, just as before and my fingers move before the words fill my mind. The fingers respond, knowing before the words are barely formed, what they must create. What is this magic liaison – finger, mind and blank page?

It was the same with pen and paper – but the process was more laborious – allowed my mind to divert, suggest a different word or phrase. It would be stumble and hiccup as we went. This is smoother, effortless at times as though I am merely turning a well-oiled lock. And yet … a doubt lurks … who then is the creator?

Who then assumes the credit – if credit is to be had?

I love a blank page. Here we go again. Where are we heading? Who or what shall we find? How shall we untangle the convolutions when highways divert into byways and obstacles bar our path? It's trust – trust that leads us on, blank page and I. A partnership based on trust. Blank page opens the door and leads me in, leads me on to ever new places. And what lies ahead, where shall we find ourselves in the future?

Indeed, how long will this partnership endure, will there be a parting of the ways when I no longer sense the path? The way ahead may become obscure, and I lose my way – what then? It's too hard to think along those lines – too hard to think I may lose the way. No longer run in tandem with this freedom to uncover new delights.

Best not to think of such. Just enjoy the partnership we share, blank page and I.

WHERE HAVE YOU BEEN?

Keeping as still as possible, the sun beating down on the back of his head, Harry watched the insect life before him. He had never thought to lie and look, really look, at what lay in and around the grass roots at his feet and if he had not dropped his gun in the undergrowth, it could have continued to be a mystery.

Gun retrieved, he let his hand rest on it as he watched the bustling world which existed probably ninety-nine per cent of the time completely unseen by mankind. Insects of all sizes and shapes bustled about, intent on their own world and needs. A shiny black beetle laboured up a stone, stopping at the top as if catching its breath. A snail drifted serenely along its personal, glistening trail which a train of ants circumnavigated by following each other up a twig, across another and down via a stone, to continue their hurried journey.

The grass was burnt yellow brown by the relentless sun, so much so that a bright green caterpillar was a vivid contrast to its background. Harry smiled as a vivid blue butterfly fluttered in a gap in the grasses – he wondered if they could possibly be related – which came first – caterpillar or butterfly?

His musing was abruptly halted by the hint of movement in the foreground; the grass stems moved, swayed. He watched. Sure enough, something was ahead of him. Moving. His hand tensed on the gun as he held his breath.

There it was again; the suggestion almost of something just ahead. And then his eyes caught a glimpse of the striped body. He waited, heart thudding in his ears. A tiger, moving so cautiously as to be almost motionless. Was it stalking? What had it seen? Had it detected his presence? Seemingly not - as slowly, so very slowly, it moved on, cautious step by cautious step. He saw the stripes merge, disappear, the grasses ceased their swaying but still he dare not move. Not yet.

Then, feeling the immediate danger had passed, he wondered where to go. Retrace his steps? … move off slowly in pursuit? … and decided to head for higher ground. He knew the ground rose sharply on his right. From up there he might be able to see where the tiger was heading.

Firmly holding his gun in his right hand, he edged

forward on hands and knees, wincing slightly as sharp stones dug into his bare knees, until the terrain gave way to softer earth, where a trickle of water hinted at an almost dried up water course. Seizing the opportunity, Harry dug his left hand into the mud and wiped it across his face. Once he stood up, he knew his face would blend in more easily into the shadows among the growth up the mountainside. But for now, he continued on hands and knees.

It seemed a long time before he felt safe enough to stand upright and peer down through the vegetation to the clearing below. It was a mixture of relief and excitement as he spotted the tiger far below. It was still stalking forward, belly low, foot following foot in slow motion and he could now see its quarry.

A fat brown bear, seemingly oblivious of approaching danger, was placidly sitting in a patch of sunlight for all the world as if it were sunbathing. Tiger crept on. Should he shout? Fire? But he hated killing, the gun was merely for his protection.

It was too late. Tiger was tensing, tip of tail switching from side to side, and then it leapt. Its body arced high before landing on the bear, a moment of suspended animation and tiger bounced off again and flashed into the undergrowth. Bear, knocked sideways, lay motionless with an expression of bewildered surprise.

Harry stepped forward, out from the shadows - could he risk running forward? Bear did not move. Could not be dead? Would the tiger return – was that part of its devious plan? Whirling thoughts, undecided, a moment of hesitation and Harry missed his footing. He slipped, grabbed at, and missed a nearby branch and fell, slipping and rolling down the mountainside. Boulders cascaded around him as he fell. He landed all too quickly, gun wrenched from his grasp, not far from the bear.

Battling for breath and desperately trying to gather his thoughts, Harry was all too aware of the proximity of the bear, the possibility of the tiger's return even as a shadow darkened the sky above. A vulture, circling slowly.

No gun. His eyes searched for a nearby heavy stone – could he hit the vulture from here? Would he alarm the bear into retaliation? Bears were usually peaceful animals if not hungry he thought, but after the tiger's attack would it be in a disgruntled mood? So many questions and no stone nearby. Bear and he lay in silence before the vulture seemingly lost interest, circled once more before moving on.

And the tiger had not returned.

Or was it watching events? Biding its time? Rolling over onto all fours, Harry slowly crept to the left keeping one eye on the bear, which appeared to have resumed its interrupted meditations, until he reached the edge of the jungle. With his back to a large tree, he debated whether to return up the mountainside in an effort to locate his gun, when he sensed he was being watched.

Glancing swiftly left and right, he saw nothing untoward, but the uneasy fear grew. Something, somewhere was watching. Watching and waiting.

The faintest of hint of a rustle – he glanced up and there was the tiger on the branch directly above, tip of tail twitching, its yellow eyes glaring downwards, claws tensing on the branch.

And he ran. He ran.

He ran, mindless, heedless of undergrowth, branches whipping back into his face, tearing at his clothes.

Ran until winded and falling through the open door …

into the kitchen where his mother paused, iron in hand,

'Harry! Have you been up on that rockery again? I told you to keep off while I left the hosepipe running – if you have damaged any of the new plants … and just look at the state of you! that's the second shirt you've torn the buttons off this week – what are you doing out there? And I hope you haven't left any toys outside again – it looks like a storm is coming. Last time it was your teddy bear which got soaked and took ages to dry out. For goodness sake, go and wash your face while I feed Tibby.'

Harry watched as the sleek tabby cat slid through the door and sat by the fridge, a secretive smile on its face.

Oh for the happy days of childhood and make believe

CRISP

'Do stand still, child,' that was from Great Aunt Grace.

'Pretty as a picture,' that was Great Aunt Rose.

I stood quite still being pretty as a picture but hoped it wouldn't be for too long, both petticoats were stiffly starched as well as my new cotton dress and the crisp ruffles round my neck already tickled and scratched.

Both Great Aunts stood back, looking at me, one critically, the other fondly.

'Now just remember the tea party is a most special occasion. Most special. We are celebrating the engagement of your Aunt Victoria and her fiancé Charles. He is a most respectable gentleman, well thought of in the bank and this tea party is a most serious occasion. Most serious. His parents will be here too for the first time. You are expected to be seen, but not heard of course. Seen to be a credit to the family ...'

Great Aunt Grace would have gone on for ever but was interrupted by the sound of the rat-a-tat-tat of the door knocker.

The hustle and bustle rose to a crescendo and I was able to slip away into the background. It was all very well for people to talk about 1900 being the turn of the century and the start of a whole new era but as far as I could see, nothing much would change for seven-year-old girls. Not if Great Aunt Grace had anything to do with it.

I walked out onto the terrace, it was a little cooler outdoors, which was a blessing and I stood looking down the garden, not daring to sit and crease my crisply starched dress. The murmured greetings drifted through the French doors, everyone sounding so delighted to be here, so pleased to meet each other. I wished I were back home on the farm with my parents, but they had said this invitation, this visit, would be a great experience. Well, it was. But not quite the way I had hoped.

There wasn't much time to dwell on these thoughts. I was called in to meet and greet the guests. Fiancé Charles was a great disappointment. My Aunt Victoria was so pretty that I had expected her fiancé to be tall and handsome, but here was a short, rather stout, man with a horrid moustache, whose hands were sweaty and held on to my hand just that bit too long when we were introduced.

To my dismay the Great Aunts and Aunt Victoria declared that before tea, Charles' mother should see some materials which had just been delivered .... So suitable for a special sort of dress. Such a special sort of dress, gentlemen should not be allowed to see. Charles' father promptly settled himself with The Times and before I knew it, Charles announced that his pretty little new niece-to-be could escort him round the garden.

So off we went.

Charles strolled along swinging his cane as we walked down the gravel path and round the flower beds, through the gate and round the vegetable garden, coming back through the shrubbery. He didn't seem to need much in the way of conversation for which I was grateful, and I looked forward to getting back into the house, and perhaps then I would be excused.

All at once he put his arm round me and pulled me close, leaned down saying hoarsely, 'How about a kiss for your new uncle?'

My new dress! So fresh and crisp. It would be crumpled. Without thinking I pushed hard and fled along the path.

I was glad it was his white flannels which had muddy marks 'because he'd tripped'.

I couldn't have faced Great Aunt Grace if it had been my fresh crisp dress.

BAD PENNY

Uncle Oswald never gave me one. Or if he did Mr Jones never noticed. I'm sure he would have done if there was one - because I spend all my pocket money there. So, there couldn't have been.

A bad penny I mean.

Uncle Oswald (he told me to call him Ozzie, said he didn't care for all the uncle malarkey), but when I tried it out Aunt Charlotte said I wasn't to call him that name – she meant Ozzie – and not to use common language – she meant malarkey. Aunt Charlotte is really my Great Aunt, but she says we can dispense with the Great Aunt part when we are merely having a conversation. But not to say Ozzie. (Seems illogical to me – that's one of my new words, illogical; Mr Smythe at school says we should always use a new word ten times every day for three days. That way it becomes embedded, he says).

Well, anyway, they always whispered 'bad penny' whenever they talked about him – Ozzie I mean – and they seemed to be always talking about him. That's Aunt Charlotte and Uncle Simon – though he is really Great Uncle Simon because he's married to Great Aunt Charlotte. And Aunt Elizabeth - she's really an aunt and not Great at all because she's my mother's sister. We always spend the summer holiday together at the Old House – that's where Grandma and Grandpa live but we all share it in the summer and lots of other uncles and aunts come to stay for weekends or when they can.

But there's not many cousins and none for me to play with because they (the cousins) are all Old. If they are not up at Varsity, they are getting ready for it and do a lot of swotting and mocks with tutors. I'm the Last One, they say. (Varsity is really university but they never say that. But I can't say Ozzie).

It's the first time I've met Ozzie – he's never been here before – at least, not that I remember. But he must have been here because he's a sort of grandson and he showed me where he used to climb out of the nursery window and on to the crenelated bit (that's my second new word this week, crenelated) in the afternoons when he wanted to go down to play with the village boys on the green.

Ozzie said it's quite easy if you don't look down. He says all manner of things and I'm not altogether sure that I believe all of them, but he does spin a good yarn and he's always interested in what I'm doing and what I think about things. He says that I relieve the boredom of conventionality. He said that after I showed him how I don't have to climb out of the nursery window, I just wait till they are all having their naps and then I go out by the side door because Annie leaves it open for her follower, Bert, (he comes in the afternoons if he comes – sometimes Annie looks sad and sniffs a lot and says Bert must have been busy). And Cook says, 'Just as well' and then she sniffs.

And I'm quite sure Ozzie doesn't have bad pennies – usually he gives me a half crown but once or twice he has pulled out a handful of change and given me a lot of odd coins because he hasn't got a half crown. I don't mind at all because each time it came to more than half a crown. And all the pennies must have been good because I spent them all.

My mother likes Ozzie as well – though she has reminded me not to say Ozzie at the table or when we are all together. But then I don't say very much at all because little boys aren't supposed to interrupt, and they all talk so much I can't. Unless somebody asks me a question, which they don't usually. I've seen them walking in the greenhouses (Mother and Ozzie), they like all the plants and stop and look at them a lot. Which is nice because nobody else seems to take any interest in the greenhouses and Mr McFarlane works very hard even though he looks grumpy and once told me he didn't know why he made the effort. But he didn't say effort for what and when I asked, he told me he couldn't remember.

Anyway, I thought I'd go down to the village one afternoon when they're all asleep, so I looked for Ozzie. Found him in the greenhouse with my mother looking at the plants again. I said I was thinking about going down to the village – they don't mind me talking. Expect that's because they don't talk very much when they are looking at the plants. Sometimes they are so quiet you would never think anyone was in there unless you went and looked behind the big fig tree at the end.

My mother said, 'Remember to put your hat on' but she smiled, and I know she doesn't mind when I forget. Ozzie said, 'How about a bit of extra finance?' and pulled a handful of change out of his pocket. 'No half-crowns today', he said and poured a pile of coins into my hands. I said, 'Thank you very much Ozzie' and looked at the coins. A few were pennies, they looked all right to me. But I'd wondered if a bad penny went bad and a bit soft like an apple, so I lifted one up and bit it. Hard. It was not bad.

They were both staring at me, so I said I was testing to see if it was a bad penny. It was very quiet in the greenhouse, just one of the taps dripping at the end. My mother looked very pink; Ozzie started laughing. He said, 'Cut along Benjamin before Mr Jones sells all the toffee apples. As I went off, I heard him say, 'Nothing changes.' He's wrong of course, I don't care for toffee apples now and am investigating the value of liquorice torpedoes for tupppence and nougat for a penny ha'penny – but it's all in one block so you can't make it last as long as when you suck one at a time.

And I'm writing this down because Mr Smythe says if you write something down it helps you understand and remember it. I don't know if it will, but am writing it down anyway to put in my treasure box and I'll hide it under the loose squeaky floorboard behind the rocking horse. And then when I come back it will be there to help me remember this summer. And if we don't come back because Africa is a long way away … then another little boy might find it and know where I am and why.

Ozzie and my mother are going to get married, and we are all going to go live in Africa. Ozzie says he has a big farm and life is exciting every day and we shall be free. Aunt Charlotte said, 'Free? What is free?' and Uncle Simon made that snorty sound and said, 'If you survive all the mosquitoes.'

There was a lot of shouting about Ozzie being a bad penny – he didn't have *any*, he was *one* They said. They asked my mother how she could contemplate marriage with a bounder who'd taken his share and gone off into the unknown. He should have invested it all in Grandpa's Bank and kept it in the family like all the family did.

Everybody talked – and shouted – such a lot I can't write it all down. But Ozzie isn't a proper uncle – a side shoot Uncle Simon shouted, only a side shoot – so he and my mother can be married. But They are most cross because Mum and Ozzie are taking me.

It's all very mixed up. My father was the eldest, so the Big House and Bank are my father's tail and he died so they are my tail now. I haven't GOT one, a tail, but the Big House and Bank are in my tail. They say.

They sound all mixed up; but it seems we can go off to Africa and see elephants walk on Ozzie's farm and grow lots of cotton and tobacco, but we can come back when we want because it's all in my tail.

And this is the end of my tale, not my *tail*!

THERE CAN BE NO DOUBT

No. There was never any doubt. Everyone knew that Percy spent a good part of every day, rain or shine, sitting on the low wall by the stream which ran through the village. The low wall ran along the roadside where the stream disappeared into a culvert under the road, to reappear on the other side, before meandering alongside the back garden of The Swan.

Most of the time the stream was gently burbling – a phrase much used by those of a poetic turn of mind. But on occasion it could be termed a raging torrent and would thrash itself along the banks as it turned the bend approaching the culvert under the road. Again, perhaps a poetic phrase. And as we are talking about Percy probably not entirely relevant; for no one ever thought of Percy and poetry. Of course, being that sort of small … basic… stuck in the mud (often literally) … mundane type of village, poetry did not feature much in conversation much less pursuits.

Returning to Percy – easily done for he rarely ventured

far and once ensconced on the wall would be there for hours – people had stopped wondering what the attraction was. In fact, some would have confessed to assuming there was no attraction, apart from the wall being of an eminently suitable height and when warmed by the sun, the old stone was remarkably comfortable. I suppose what I am saying, in a roundabout sort of way, is that Percy sat on the wall, and no one was interested why.

He was old – and that in itself meant he was largely unnoticed. Old people, no matter how interesting and relatively energetic, are frequently unnoticed or ignored – until they fall down in awkward places at inconvenient times. Or create some other unusual diversion. (My uncle Toby is a case in point, having acquired a set of bagpipes and after a rather secretive week away to acquire the basic skills, chose to attempt to emulate one of his heroes – the piper who played for Queen Victoria every morning. Aunt Matilda said it was not grounds for divorce, merely murder and if she had not tripped over her nightgown there might very well have been…) But I am wandering from the point.

 So, we have established Percy was old. And reticent. No, I haven't mentioned that yet. it's just that everyone knew he didn't talk – at least not much and certainly not often. No matter what time of day you passed over the bridge, Percy would be sitting on the low wall, worn in comfortable dips and hollows by wind and rain and the frequent tramp of children's feet. For it was almost a rite of passage that every child would walk along the low wall once it had mastered the art of walking and in some instances, escaping from over-anxious maternal hands. And for the next few years, those children could not pass that way without walking along the wall. Hesitantly perhaps at first, then with increasing bravado and with time would even pause, bend and peer down into the rippling waters.

At such times, Percy would stand up, flexing his knees a little and nod down at the intrepid traveller as he (or she) passed. He was never inclined to comment but appeared to enjoy the momentary diversion before resuming his seat and placid gaze at the stream and overhanging willow.

And that's how it was. And would have continued.

But then I made the exciting and amazing discovery that people were paid to write. Now hold on. I was young, very young. And I suppose should admit that I was prone to have 'my nose in a book' (my mother's phrase) and also inclined to be a bit of a dreamer. How else could one not be – once I'd learned to read (an automatic skill which ran alongside breathing or so it seemed) and immersed myself in all those wonderful adventure stories – Robinson Crusoe, Masterman Ready, The Borrowers, Tom and the Water Babies as stepping stones to Jane Eyre and Wuthering Heights, Count of Monte Cristo and the Man in the Iron Mask …

Late in life (I was ten and in top class) it was something of a shock – but delight – to begin to understand that not only could I continue to scribble away at my stories, for that is how Authors, Proper Writers, must have started. Just possibly I could do the same. When approached, my father gave me probably the only relevant and practical advice ever; 'Think on,' he said, 'they all had to start somewhere …. Small …. Probably writing bits for newspapers …'

As this more or less coincided with Mrs Matthews introducing a Class Newspaper – not only that but also nominating me as Editor for the first half term, my ambitions knew no boundaries. Editor! But only for half a term. I had to make my mark!

Very rapidly I learnt the art of delegating - school news, crossword, painting competition, How to Make a Dress (for a doll) etc - and cast my mind about for something more - sensational - impressive - relevant to the village

- unknown to anyone else. And somehow fell upon the idea of Live Interviews. I would interview well known Personalities in the village.

Therein lay the rub.

Who was a Well-Known Personality?

There was the vicar – rather unapproachable and would, I knew, be more inclined to question my disappearance from church once Sunday School had lost its charm (the book prizes for Good Attendance did not keep pace with my literary tastes).

The owner of the village drapers – I considered the boring hours spent in there while my mother deliberated over materials and threads and bias binding and … besides he smelt strongly of mints and tobacco – not a pleasant mix.

The doctor – would I dare? How? Would one make an appointment and then admit not to a cough or ache but proffer instead a list of questions in lieu of ailments? Somehow, I thought that was not the right approach but lacked the courage to present myself at his front door 'out of hours'.

The owner of The Swan – now he must have an interesting life – meet so many people – hear so many stories … No. Could not do that. It meant stepping over the threshold of A Pub. Absolute dens of iniquity according to my mother, who would not answer any questions about such places. They existed in books I read and sounded interesting … full of character – think of Jim and The Black Spot in Treasure Island. But somehow real-life pubs in our village (we had two - The Swan and Queen o' T'Owd Thatch, which had a very pretty thatched roof) were not to be part of my life.

It didn't really make sense. My Mother had told me about the time that they, as school children, had been marched down the village High Street to stand in front of The Swan to cheer and wave flags when Queen Mary was at the hunt meet. So, it was OK for Queen Mary to be outside – and perhaps she had been INSIDE? – but not me. There might be pictures or mementoes of that momentous day hanging on the walls. Perhaps the landlord knew some history of the day.

Sitting on the wall, on the warmed stone, I looked at The Swan and wondered what delights, what information lay inside. And sighed. And sadly, looked about me for inspiration. Inspiration there was none. Only Percy sitting a bit further along, seated as usual midway and gazing absently at the trailing willow leaves bobbing in the water.

Would Percy know anything about the Day when Queen Mary rode with the hunt? He was old, even if he hadn't been there, he might have heard stories. I slipped off the wall and scuffling my Clarks sandals in the dust, edged my way along until I was just by his left elbow. Stood still. And gazed down into the water.

Now how and why I will never know.

But after a while we got into conversation. Percy and me.

I think … think I started talking about the Class Newspaper and how I thought the Landlord would have stories about Queen Mary's visit. Percy didn't give the impression of listening – or at least of being interested. And after a while my regretful chatter died away. And I found myself sitting companionably on the wall beside Percy just watching the water. For the first time I saw that instead of being brown as I'd always thought, the water was quite clear and as I watched, I could see small fish darting to and fro in the currents. Minnows I guessed. Not as attractive or desirable as sticklebacks, which we always hoped to find on fishing expeditions armed with nets and jam jars.

It was warm on the wall and Percy was good company; didn't go on about how I'd grown and how was school – in the way most adults did, when you knew the very next thing was that they would tell you that school days were the very best days of your life.

Not if you can't interview a Personality I thought sulkily and swung my legs over so that they were dangling over the water, and I could peer down better.

Percy suddenly held a hand out. And then put it back down on his knee. And cleared his throat.

I looked up at him. 'Be careful,' he said.

'Oh, I will,' I said. 'Anyway, it's not deep.'

'Nay, it's not deep now … but when it is …' he shook his head slowly.

Curious, I asked, 'Have you ever seen it VERY deep?'

Then, very slowly, in fits and starts, with pauses as if he were reliving the time, Percy told me. Told me how long ago, one winter, a long hard winter with deep snow which melted and contributed to the deepening waters in the stream and how the swollen beck (as old villagers termed

30

the stream) had roared through the village deeper than ever before, amazing all. And how one Sunday, many had wandered down to the wall to watch it rush under the culvert and guess how far it might back up if the culvert didn't cope. And whether it would then flood back up towards and onto the road.

I could see and hear it in my mind's eye.

And hear the shouts and cries of alarm when a small boy, under the willow and rasher than his mates, fell in. More shouts and cries as a man leapt into the raging torrent (a true term) and seizing the boy's jacket managed to battle back to the bank with him.

I found I was holding my breath.

Percy paused. Again. Looked down at me with watery blue eyes.

'It were your Dad. Saved my lad. And don't be thinking I can jump in after thee. But think on, that might be a story for thi newspaper.'

UTOPIA

It was an idyllic childhood.

Looking back, I'm usually thankful and smile at some of the memories. But I must admit, sometimes I wonder what was the point, what was it all about, was it worth it?

But, yes, it was. An idyllic childhood and nothing can take that away from me. A period of perfect happiness – and I didn't even know enough to wonder if it would go on for ever. My parents were wise; they still are of course. No doubt about that.

Earliest memories are of being with my parents, one or both, and playing with toys or a game or just being together and enjoying a … a walk looking at flowers … or a visit to a place where they would point out an interesting feature. They were very fond of visiting historical sites, not surprising really – they had many books about history and always enjoyed answering my questions about things I read about the past. So, I grew up familiar with topics featured in the many books they gave me. For some reason my parents seemed to like books – the paper kind rather than the E books we used when I went to TrainStat - because they would usually add that extra bit of information which made 'history come alive'. In some ways I enjoyed that more than the Living History sites we would visit on Experience trips – but I'm jumping ahead.

Having started this, after much very careful thought, I'm determined to be rational and accurate. Emotion can wait until later. Now there's an interesting thought – can I leave emotion out of this account? I have emotions – can they be detached and set aside? I mustn't be side-tracked down that detour. I meant to say - I am going to be rational, accurate and log it all in a consecutive manner. No leaping to and fro, until you don't know if you're coming or going, and explaining what I thought about it all at the time. I won't even let myself wonder if you will be there to read this, because if I let my mind think along those lines, I may be too disheartened to continue. At fourteen I should be able to be dispassionate and reflective.   And yet, fourteen is in many ways inexperienced and naïve.

So, childhood. And the happy days together. I was an only child but never felt lonely, there was always something to do, and usually someone to share it with.

Mum was more fun indoors and was always introducing me to a new idea or activity – but they both did. Dad was the outdoorsy one really – the garden was constantly changing and evolving as he introduced new plants or new activities. I had a jungle gym which grew with me over the years – from a very simple climbing frame and swing to a complicated structure. Nothing was ever taken away, just added to – so as my circle of friends grew there was a part which appealed to every age, and we could be quite a mixed group.

That was the one way in which my parents were different, although it never occurred to me at the time. Mum showed me how to cook using different ingredients – it took me a long time to notice that my friends' mums didn't seem to do that. It was a click and accept delivery. Mum did that too – a great time saver, ordering meals – so, yes, she sometimes did it too. We went shopping of course, you do, don't you? But Mum would sometimes even buy food items in a shop instead of just ordering. And, as I said, she would cook them to make a meal; eventually I could do it too, but never as good as her. I remember her laughing, saying, 'Fina, you'll never be a chef '– and then having to explain 'chef'.

And Dad made things (he cooked a few times too I remember but it wasn't often) – he was good at making things with his hands. Yes, cooking is with your hands … I'm not explaining things very well. It's just how I remember. Dad made things – things to play with, like a toy train I could pull or push across the floor. He showed me pictures in a book, pictures of a steam engine long ago and read to me how people travelled on them. And how goods were transported; he took ages explaining why and what and where. My train had both coaches and wagons, so I could say it was a passenger or a goods train.

His friends admired my train, they asked him how and why he liked making it. But none of them made one. Carla and Billi had trains after I got mine, but theirs were Click ones. Carla's dad ordered her a bright red one, Billi's was a metallic blue. Mine was authentic black, Dad said. We were friends then, Andi and Billi, Carla and Dina … and more.

We had met sometimes when our mothers got together and drank tea, but we met every day once we were old enough to start Training. That was exciting - my first day at Training. Exciting for all of us I guess, putting on the uniform, saying goodbye to our parents, going into TrainStat for the first time. Mum had read me stories about the old days when children went to school, and we looked at the pictures together. I couldn't understand why they were different, in different books. Mum said the schools had different types of buildings (they were even different ages!) and some had uniforms and some didn't – but the uniforms were different in different schools (I asked her why but she said she couldn't say). It was interesting but very confusing. It's so much simpler for us today, the TrainStats are all built the same way, our uniforms are all the same green – except for the number on our backs. I was in TrainStat 3 and had a black 3 on the back of my top, when I moved on to TestStat 3 it was a 3 with a circle round it.

Mum said she couldn't remember when schools changed to Training Stations and Testing Stations. But I was saying how excited I was – I remember walking in through the big glass doors in my green uniform and meeting my Trainer for the first time. Andi and Carla were walking in at the same time, Billi and Dina were already there. There were twenty of us altogether and I knew most of them already; mums often drank tea together and some dads used to come to watch my Dad make things.

Trainer said we were going to enjoy practising things together. 'It's all very well knowing things and being able to do things, but we all have to practise how to do them well and easily. And most of all, practise doing them well together. 'Together' is a most important word.'

And she was right, it was fun, we did enjoy practising together. It was strange how we could all do something – but never quite the same. But the more we practised, the more we got to do it in the same way and at the same speed until Trainer would shout, 'Well done, my friends - that was identical!' It was fun. Although the physical things were the hardest, in the end I could keep up with my friends. Everything else … the reading and exploring the Net, writing reports and analysing data, comparing statistics and creating art forms were of course fun and easy. After all, that's what computers are for, to do the work.

We were all friends together and as time went on Andi, Billi, Dina and me were usually together when we had to do things in groups. Trainer said we could all really think and collaborated well together; she seemed a bit surprised as she was adding the data to our records. Not that that mattered one bit; all that mattered was that we could complete tasks and watch her click away on screen. As time went on the tasks were progressively more complicated of course and we were proud of the glowing boxes on our records.

But we were all friends, every one of us and when we had birthdays, we would all be together, and our parents would gather round watching us as we played games.

Trainer would be there too of course, talking with our parents. That's how times have changed; Trainer was with us all the way through TrainStat. Long ago when children went to school they had teachers – and a different one every year! Just imagine, we said, a different one every year.

So, if you asked me what I remember about my time in TrainStat, I can tell you about the things we learnt to do and what we practised together and alone – but you know that. You must have been through the system, and you have done the same things in the same way. And you know it was a fun and happy time. Of course, we went on several Experience trips, like you do.

It was fascinating (Yes, fascinating not just interesting) to watch and participate in a Living Experience; I wasn't so keen on Medieval – too cold and messy, Anglo Saxons after the Romans were better, but Tudors were my favourite – the costumes! But I could not forget the living conditions were still so primitive. The notion of actually living like that day after day became depressing after the novelty wore off and I'd be relieved when Trainer switched off and the set went into suspended animation.

When Mum and Dad had shared history books or stories about long ago with me, I'd had a sort of envy – it looked so interesting. There was … oh …. I don't know … so much more variety in everything. That's it. Variety. But of course, as I learnt more at the Experience Stations, I saw how simple, easy and better controlled our lives are in comparison. And we are so much the better for it. No more hard, physical labour – it is odd to think how people actually did physical work in fields and factories – even offices. Trainer laughed as she said, 'They actually invented the first computers and the first robots - and then continued doing all the work themselves! '

Experience Trips were interesting but sad. Sad that people long ago had had such difficulties understanding the world and had continued the damage even when they understood what was causing global warming and how natural resources could not last for ever. Couple that with expanding populations. Even as young children we could understand that it could not be allowed to continue. Children used to work down coal mines! Yes, times had changed, and we had progressed. There was no more illness so no more suffering.

Only one tiny little thing was different, and I didn't even recognise it as such at the time. It's only now that it registers as … different.

When we were about seven Billi came to school one

day and showed us the gap where a tooth had been … told us that our teeth fall out and a new one grows in its place. Trainer explained about first and second teeth; it was all quite logical. And one by one my friends lost first one tooth and then another. And then one day I had a loose tooth that wobbled a bit in my mouth - and it hurt more when I wiggled it with my tongue. I told Mum it was sore, and she said I had a loose tooth, and it would fall out … and asked me why I looked surprised. I said nobody had said it would hurt when it happened. She thought for a minute, then said I should be sensible and brave and not talk about it. Brave, yes. Sensible, why? She looked very tired and told me 'Fina, just try to be sensible and brave.' So, I was. I went to TrainStat and when my tongue bumped my tooth, I didn't say 'Ouch!' If my friends had all kept quiet about it being sore, then I would too. To be honest, I was thinking more about the tooth fairy! We might have better and more developed lives but there was a place for tradition.

And that was the only thing I remember being - what? Unexpected?

As I said earlier, it was an idyllic childhood. TrainStat was fun and a challenge and in addition to that, there were our holidays. Dad and Mum and me used to go camping – every time Dad would say, 'Time to get away' and Mum would be making lists before he'd finished the sentence. We'd take the second quadcopter and Dad used to say. 'Are you going to pack everything?' and Mum would say, 'You never know …' I must say it was fun to live with so little and yet we always seemed to have everything we needed. Mum often said that we could always pop over to a Settlement, but Dad was insistent getting away was getting away from everything.

So, we camped in forests and high on hills and down in deep valleys, by rivers and lakes and once by the sea. Though we never repeated that holiday; I couldn't be specific, couldn't put my finger on it and memory can play tricks. All I can say is that I felt in some odd way it was a sad holiday. No, not sad. That's not the right word. Perhaps … quieter than usual. Reflective? were my parents quieter? No matter. We had holidays every year and they were always Great!

Once or twice when I was very young, I asked a friend or two what did they do on holiday – I mean everybody went away on holiday. But they didn't say much – just that it was a good experience or something similar. It made me feel almost intrusive and then I thought how fortunate I was to always have such great times with my folks.

And so, we come to TestStat. Bigger and better. That's what you expect in life, things get bigger and better. Perhaps not a very clear way to describe it but you know what I mean. When you are small, your horizons and expectations are correspondingly small but as you grow and develop so do your expectations and experiences. And so it was. Of course, moving from TrainStat to TestStat we had a new Trainer, he too was very encouraging. But you know what, we all went on together, making progress all the time. Initially.

Then diversity came into our lives. Some of us were better suited to other things ... it was never specified in any detail ... just some of us would be diverted on to a new course ... and disappear. This new course (or courses – were there more than one?) were never at our TestStat. I asked my mother once if the new courses were far away because I never saw Gella again after she left for her new course. I thought it might be like the boarding schools I'd read about in the old days for she was never anywhere about. Mum said vaguely she didn't really know. I thought it must be very far away and hoped I wouldn't get diverted. Mum said I shouldn't worry about that and perhaps not to talk about it.

Later, over time, Harri and Lona were diverted – not at the same time. They never came back either. And it wasn't very long – don't ask me how long – at that age you don't register dates as important much less make a note – just later, some time later, I saw that Gella's mum had a new baby. A girl. And later Harri and Lona's mums had new babies, one a boy and one a girl. I saw them at school events when their parents came along – for Gella's older brother.

Apart from that TestStat was fine; my record had a row of glowing boxes. Trainer always looked pleased with me; sometimes it seemed a mix of pleased and surprised.

And very slowly I began to notice other things. Silly trivial little things. When you say to yourself Oh?… or Why? … but it's never big enough or easy to put into words. And if I write them down it will look silly or perhaps it demonstrates how slow and stupid I was. But when life is normal and happy and safe and everyone about you is happy and normal, what is there to think about? to wonder about?

Like I said, Mum and her friends would go to each other's houses 'for coffee' or 'to tea' and as we grew older, we went along less often. But not before I noticed that very few other houses had paper books like ours. Things had never been 'made'. Mum made biscuits and little cakes and mini sandwiches, and her friends would always say

'How very clever' and 'You are so original'; you would think Mum would have been flattered but she would smile while all the time her eyes would be sad. And Dad's friends would ask him to show how he'd take a cutting from a bush to grow into a new one, how he had made me a model working windmill; he always smiled as he demonstrated but I began to notice that sometimes he too would sound just a bit tired. Or bored?

Were my parents getting old? Were they older than I thought they were? I said, it all sounds so trivial.

And so trivial in the middle of life that it was shelved, put aside.

There was one other incident— at TestStat one day, Billi and I were walking down some steps and as I hurried down the lower steps, I tripped and went sprawling down on to the gravel below. And landed with quite a thump. Rolled over, sat up and saw blood welling up from the sore graze on my knee. Billi was standing looking down at me with a look of shock on his face. 'I'm OK,' I said. 'It looks worse than it is,' but he just stood and stared. Fortunately, just then Trainer came down the steps, saw me and said quickly, 'It's fine Billi, just fine. You go ahead, I'll take care of Fina.' Billi walked off quickly. Trainer took me into his office and washed my knee, it

45

soon stopped bleeding, but he said I should go home for the rest of the day and actually phoned Mum.

Her quadcopter landed within a few minutes and off we flew. Mum had some cream which eased the stinging and there wasn't much of a mark next day. And I was back at TestStat of course – couldn't bear to miss a special day.

For the next day was a busy one when we were due to test the design programmes we had been working on for weeks. All went well. Like it always did, although the way Trainer talked, we often had some doubts. Secretly I think it was just his way to spur us on. Like I said, all went well but that was the first time I noticed a few people were looking at me - but looked away when they saw me watching. Some were just giving me a sort of sidelong puzzled look. Trainer pointed out that my design worked the quickest and smoothest but that was hardly enough to warrant the … the curious looks. Yes, that was it. Some were giving me curious looks. Perhaps they had thought I could never be the best and first in something. Perhaps they all thought they were better than me.

We would finish TestStat when we were fifteen and move on to Placement. Placement is where life gets really exciting. Well, I thought it sounded exciting. That's probably when I became really aware that I was different.

Everyone was so matter of fact. So bloody matter of fact. They didn't talk about Placement – you know how when a big change is coming you speculate about the ifs and buts and Can you? Do you? Is there? When do?

Oh, my goodness, I had so many questions, but no one was in the least bit interested. We would finish TestStat and move on to Placement and then move into our own homes with a partner. And no one mentioned it, no one speculated or suggested or... anything!

Oh, I do hope you read this. That I can share it with somebody who understands.

So bloody matter of fact.

I knew we went through TrainStat and TestStat and then at Placement we moved on to the place of work. I mean, I wasn't stupid. I knew that all our fathers went to work, that's what they did. They went to work checking and ensuring life ran smoothly ... after all, it's obvious that the best of computers can break down, have a glitch. And then there is a malfunction in a factory or somewhere. That's what fathers did. And then they came home, and mothers had a meal ready, and the children had been cared for and then they all enjoyed some relaxing sport or activity.

You know! You know how it works.

And so, the next little step is choosing who you will lead that life with - once you've been Placed. I had my eye on Billi. We always worked well together. So, I sort of assumed. And one day when we'd (Billi and me) completed a project on an alternative design for vertiports and Trainer said we'd completed it far quicker than anyone before, I said to Billi if we were Placed together, we could spend our evenings designing more than vertiports. He just laughed and said, 'As if! As if you could be Placed with anyone!' and walked off.

That took the wind out of my sails (had just read that and loved the image – once Dad had explained it). Thought about it all the way home. Thought about it all through dinner – we were sitting round the table – until Mum said, 'What is it, Fina? What are you thinking about? '

So … so … so I told them. We'd always talked about everything, but it wasn't very easy to tell them that Billi didn't want to be Placed with me. I said that yes, I knew it was some way off but there was nothing like planning ahead, after all we were fourteen years old, and we'd always worked so well together and … and slowly I came to a halt as I watched their faces.

And that's when they told me.

That's when the nightmare began.

They say it isn't a nightmare, but I think they probably agree with me.

I can't be Placed with anyone. As if I'd want to be now - not with one of Them.

I'm a Real, an Authentic, like Mum and Dad. And we are probably the last. The last of our kind. No others have been seen or heard of for a long time.

So, I'm most likely writing this to myself because there is probably no one out there who can read this and understand. No one else in the whole wide world who can understand me. How bloody scary is that?

Why am I doing it? To make it real to me?

Mankind was heading into oblivion. Nations had been on the verge of war for centuries. Pandemics and conflict were wiping out swathes of population just as enormous progress developing Artificial Intelligence was being made, safeguards were relaxed in the haste to compensate. Too late to recognise the madness now.

A.I., given greater freedom, created more - and more - advanced robots – so useful when mankind was so reduced.

And such was the relief that no one, NO ONE, No One at all foresaw their coming predicament. Some say that A.I. found robots so much easier to produce, guide, control … they were long term more economic (they don't get ill, and a robot production unit can produce more as some wear out) that mankind was allowed to die out. Why spend millions on medical research to keep real People alive when People robots could do everything?

Almost.

Almost but not quite.

For a long time, a line of robots had been designed to replicate humans as closely as possible – so that they would not look out of place, be obtrusive. After all, who would want a clicking metal contraption on wheels to work in your house or office? It became quite a bit of one upmanship, having the latest People design; it became harder to recognise a People model from a Real.

And that's what we are. Mum and Dad and me. My parents survived the last pandemic, they were children.

They were kept alive. Living specimens of the last of the Real People. And then they had me. Living specimens They can study - although They believe They have perfected their simulation, there is the accepted theory that perhaps Reals may one day have an original idea – some new thought, which They can adapt and assimilate. They are doubtful. In the meantime, we are interesting specimens to watch, to study, to compare.

It took a long time. Talking on into the darkness. Trying to understand, believe what I was hearing. My friends – my friends I had grown up with – had gone to TrainStat with – they were – are – ROBOTS? My same friends at TestStat? Nooooo.

But we were the same. We did the same things. Just a minute – they are robots – how come they eat and drink? How come we had birthday parties together?

It had happened gradually. As robots were replacing Real People, they were increasingly designed to blend in, belong … replace. And blending in eventually meant their design included a tract which absorbed food and drink and eliminated it much as we do. Only they did it by premeditated design. It wasn't a drawback that they couldn't actually taste anything, they merely wanted to look as though they were just like real People … shopping, eating, sharing meals, being sociable …

That I could understand – in a way. But how come my friends grew like I did? Can a People robot grow? 'Their 'holiday' was going away to be replaced with a larger model. A slightly larger model which incorporated all the information (knowledge? Ha!) and experiences from its predecessor. The People robots really worked at replicating a Real family.

The People robots pride themselves on looking and living as authentically as possible. They are a 'living' demonstration of how mankind could have been – if only we had had the sense and willpower to put in safeguards before it all went out of control.

So, my friends were robots – and so were their 'parents'?

Mum and Dad nodded. 'They really like to come to tea – they are having a 'real tea' – it is a 'real' experience,' said Mum. 'They usually only order food and go through the motions - it isn't real like mine.'

'But it's real food in the shops – we buy it – we cook it – we eat it,' I cried.

'Yes, they order food – usually ready meals – they don't

want to go to too much trouble often – and they sit down to have a meal together as a family. Because they are living the experience of being us.'

'But you say they are not?' I almost screamed. 'Not us, not real?'

Dad put his arm round me and said softly, 'No, Fina. No, they are not real like us. They like to watch us, to imitate us, but they can't be us. Remember your train? I made it because we enjoyed reading stories about trains long ago – trains that our forefathers invented, made and used. I wanted to make you happy –.'

'You did! I remember.' I interrupted.

'Billi's father got him one because he saw yours and he wanted Billi to have the same experience as you did. But it could never be the same experience – you watched me make it, compared it with the one in the book. I could tell you that your REAL great great grandparents would have REALLY travelled on REAL trains. It is part of our history. Billi's father wanted Billi to have a train, so he Clicked. Job done.'

'But if they know you are Real, they know about me?'

'We are kept as a living Real Experience, they like to watch us, imitate us in some things, but they don't understand us. When you were born, it was decided to let you live and play with the others as part of the experiment. To see how you compare.'

We sat in silence for a long time.

My head was spinning, trying to absorb and understand, make sense of what I was hearing.

'You surprised us all; Trainer thought you would not cope. But we knew things would change eventually. When you fell and Billi saw your knee bleeding, Trainer had to explain to your friends – they can't bleed of course. When you first started TrainStat we had already had meetings to discuss how your life would be handled.'

We sat on in silence.

Shock. I knew the word; characters in books had shocks, described how they felt. If you asked me how I felt right back then, I think the only word which describes it is 'isolation'. I was alone, terrifyingly alone and totally isolated.

'I think Fina should have her first glass of wine,' said

Mum.

That was some time ago. Much has happened since then.

We had always been close, Mum, Dad and me. But now we are a closely interwoven one unit. One unit against Them. Mum said I'm not to think like that, but I do. Dad said They are as much victims of misfortune as we are. He said, given freedom to programme and develop they would naturally have programmed for their progress and survival – even when it was at the expense of ours, the Real people.

In a sense it is perhaps due to our forefathers' initial lack of foresight.

Here we are, a small, controlled population in a self-sustaining area. When one of Them wears out or develops a fault, that one is replaced. Amazingly complex technology has enabled Them to replicate us. Rather sad, Dad says, that they do not have the original creative ability to design a completely new way to exist. They don't require food supplies as such, although they continue to have farms to continue the lifestyle.

(Lifestyle … but they are not alive. Or are They? They exist and function – is that alive? Alive like Meeee – a living breathing person).

Living (existing) peacefully and not expanding means this can continue indefinitely. The world is an immense place, could there be other small pockets of populations? Dad says it's a topic of conversation which has arisen a few times. The general consensus is that probably not – nothing has ever been heard – but as an idea it has not been ruled out completely. Once, long ago, attempts were made to contact any other settlements or developed areas, but nothing was heard or found. 'Since then,' Mum concluded, 'the feeling is that if there is something somewhere, contact may be made with us. Until then we just continue as we are. Living in our own little Utopia. We don't get ill – there are no diseases. We can't wear out like they do. And like everyone, we are safe.'

Which cheered me up until later.

Lying in bed, reflecting on our conversation, Mum's comment 'We can't wear out' came back to haunt me. No, indeed, we can't wear out - but I have read enough to know that eventually we die. We die, not wear out. But when Mum and Dad die, they can't be replaced with new ones. And I will be alone. Even more alone.

HE SMILED SLOWLY

He smiled slowly and my heart turned over.

I knew, even as I glanced sideways, that no one else was looking, no one else saw. And I knew it was just for me. And I smiled back, then looked down at my book as the tell-tale blush spread up my neck. Let my hair hang forward to shield my cheeks. Told myself to breathe slowly in … and out … in … and out … until my heart stopped somersaulting.

And all the while his voice never stumbled or stopped, just carried on until '… and summing up, he was a controversial figure throughout his life and his career. His personal life need not interest us – I have always been intrigued myself by the story that he rowed a boat about on the river Thames so that he could not be counted on that year's census. Hmm, time is running out. Read, Google, what you will, but above all have your essays in Monday week and find – no, *make* the time! and visit the exhibition – goodness knows when we shall next be blessed with such an opportunity in our small backwater.'

And he snapped shut the book had been holding, lifted his briefcase onto the desk and made ready to leave the room.

We, perforce, had to stay where we were.

He would be gone in a moment.

Desperately I tried to think of a question – a comment – but all that came to mind was a jumble – oh, my God, he glanced down and smiled again as he passed my desk and was through the door. The blush began again, wavered and subsided, helped by my bending to place my art notebook in my bag and rummage about for the French textbook and notebook.

The next forty minutes of Mauriac's preoccupation with family and family relationships passed me by; I made notes automatically – dead easy as Madame taught much by dictation so one half of the mind noted and recorded and the other half …

The other half remembered and reviewed the moment I glanced up and realised he was looking at me. And that slow smile in the pause as he commented 'and summing up'. And summing up, he had been looking at me – for how long? Had he been watching me as I wrote? Watched my fingers guiding the pen? I had been unaware of his gaze – though not unaware of his … his presence … his just being there … barely a couple of metres away from my desk.

Wondered if he had noticed the thin silver ring; jewellery is banned of course but keep it unobtrusive and quite often you can get away with it. For a while anyway. It was on my left hand, the hand I don't use so much, so it might not be noticed. I'd found the ring when I was helping Nan clear drawers and boxes – she has sessions of 'having a good clear out – send some of the clutter to a charity shop'. Last week I'd done some shopping for her and when I got there, she asked me to bag up the pile of stuff on her bed.

'Been having another clear out,' she'd said as she manoeuvred her walking frame through the bedroom door. 'Be a love and pack it all into a couple of bags while I put the kettle on. Fancy a cuppa?'

So, I'd folded and packed a bag full of blouses, all washed and ironed. Then the second bag took the bits of china, wrapped clumsily in newspaper, and the small box which rattled – so of course I opened it. And found the silver ring. Wasn't interested in the cuff links or the brooches. But the ring slipped on to my finger as if had always been there. And I had the quick image of his hand holding mine as he slipped the ring on my finger and then held my hand between both of his and looked into my eyes as he whispered …

'Ginger biscuits or chocolate digestive?'

And I was back in Nan's bungalow looking at the net curtains and the two bags on her bed.

Of course, I asked her if I might keep the ring and of course, she said yes. Said she had forgotten how long it had been lying about, couldn't remember when or why she had it. No matter. I had it and it was a comforting feel when I twisted it slowly on my finger and thought about the way he had been looking at me, the way he smiled oh so slowly, the way his eyebrows raised slightly when he smiled, the way that bit of hair fell forward when he was bending over , the way his thigh was outlined when he leaned over and stretched when demonstrating at an easel … oh if only my fingers could emulate with pencil what my eye knew so well.

I knew every inch of him, every movement and inflection of his voice. And I'd thought he'd not noticed me. Of course, I'd noticed him about the place, had felt that tingling as we passed on a corridor and could not believe my luck when we heard he was to take the B stream for Art in the September – had expected to be fobbed of with old Fotherdew. But the age of miracles is not past; Fotherdew left unexpectedly, new teacher, reshuffles etc etc.

 And now here I am! With him!

We still meet on corridors of course, but our closest times now are in Home Room on Mondays and the Art Room on Fridays. Home Room and the History of Art means I can listen to his voice and one day I'll think of something to say or ask when he says, 'Open for discussion …'. Some people are always ready with something to say, like the sound of their own voices, ask trivial questions. Me, I want our first exchange to be something really meaningful, make a really good impression so he will know how much I hang on his every word, how much I'm learning from him, how much he means to me.

The Art Room on the other hand, is … is … well, stressful. Got to admit it. Stressful. We're only three weeks into term so only three times in Home Room and twice in the Art Room so far and I still don't know how … where …

So far, so good. First time was a lot of time spent on rules and why, safety etc. explanations of practical work coming up and storage and recording and options. Second time he did a demo, spent a lot of time explaining and answering questions. But Friday, this Friday, we will be active, moving about, interacting. And he will be too. Any minute he will be by my side, talking about what I'm doing, asking me questions – he said he would be wanting to know why we were doing what we were doing and so on. It will be him and me, me and him, as close as can be, talking. And he might be looking at me. Will I be able to look at him? Can I stop the blushes?

Feel myself going red, skin tingles just when I think about him sometimes.

Told Nan I'd pick up the two bags on Saturday and drop them into Heart Foundation on my way into town. She offered me a fifty pee to get myself a coffee and I popped it in my pocket as I kissed her soft cheek; Mum said she likes to be independent but don't tell her how much coffee costs now. So I don't.

Walked home dreaming about Saturday. I'll pick up Nan's bags, drop them off and head for the Art Gallery. And the exhibition. He said it opens at 1000, so need to be there early and have peace and quiet to absorb the atmosphere. He has been already, there was a special View with special invitations. Pity.

Just imagine, if we just both happened to meet there …
stroll round the corner and find him - no – no – he strolls
round the corner and finds me … and I'm gazing at one
of the paintings … and don't notice him standing next to
me until he says ' You are lost in his work - like me' and
we talk a bit about the painting … and we move on to the
next one … he puts a hand just behind me to guide me
… not touching … but close … and we talk and I don't
blush and he laughs at something I say … and eventually
we have seen all the paintings and he asks if I have time
for a coffee … somehow it's not coffee … we are sitting at
a small table in a candle lit restaurant with soft music …

And I'm at the front door without knowing how I got
there, and Billy has left his scooter and football and
muddy boots just inside the front door and I trip over
them.

'Billeee!' I shout, feeling close to tears.

But at last, I'm in bed and back in the small candlelit
restaurant, turning the silver ring on my finger.

Saturday dawns bright and sunny so I can wear the pale
blue jeans with torn knees and the cotton top which
hangs off one shoulder, put on the black lacy bra – not

that you can see the lacy bits, but I know its black and lacy and … sexy. Even the strap gives a hint of what's below. I take the bus as far as Nan's and walk the rest of the way. It's not far to the charity shop and then I can walk along the High Street and by the river to the Art Gallery. I feel tall and strong and like running along, hair flowing behind me. But I don't. See a glimpse of me in Clooney's windows and pull my top a bit lower on my right shoulder. Pause as if I'm looking at the book display but check out my hair.

The steps up to the doors at the Gallery are shallow, but deep; feel I'm going hop and stop, odd feeling of being out of step. It's 1001 and the doors are open. Have never been here before and feel a bit as if I'm trespassing. It's so quiet as you go in and you can't hear the traffic behind. Very big. Seems bigger than it looks from outside. Hope my trainers don't leave a mark on the floors … so wide and shiny …

There's a poster on a board pointing to the right.

IMPRESSIONIST EXHIBITION

Don't bother to read the rest.

I'm here.

In an art gallery.

At an exhibition.

Take a deep breath and stroll round the corner. Oh, my! None … not one … of the pictures in books, photos, books let you know … prepare you for the explosion of colour and light. I stood, hardly able to breathe. So, this is why he sounded so excited, why he kept telling us we must come. To see for ourselves.

Degas. Monet. Pissarro. Renoir. Manet.

Just like he said.

There were leaflets on a small table in the middle of the room, but I didn't see them at first. Just stood in front of the first painting. And then the next. And the next. One room led into another. But I didn't want to leave this first room and walked round again. And then I noticed the table and the leaflets. And then I walked and stopped and read.

There was a man in a uniform, he came in once or twice, smiled at me and went out again. There was red rope looped along in front of the paintings – to stop you getting too close I supposed. Silly – it was far better standing back a bit. And I'd been right to come so early; there was no one else about and I had all this to myself. The leaflets helped. And I read the bit about each artist as I stood in front of each picture trying to take it all in. Wishing I understood it better. If only he could have walked round the corner – we would have had so much to talk about. Began to feel hungry, looked at my watch – midday. I'd been there two hours, two hours just walking to and fro in the three rooms, and at the end sitting in front of Manet's Le Dejeuner sur l'Herbe. That was where I felt most at home. That was me, sitting there with elbow on knee and looking slightly away as he gazes at me … it's not cold even though I'm sitting there completely naked (not a stitch, Gran would say) and he is fully dressed but I can see his eyes looking longingly as he takes a deep breath –

And a couple walk in front of me, in front of the canvas and stand there, blocking my view, dragging me back into the gallery. I realise there are low voices, another couple walk into the room and looking at my watch, I see it's one o'clock.

And I am hungry, hungry and thirsty. Decide I'll walk down to Cheery Chippy and if it's quiet, treat myself to a burger, chips and a Coke, to 'eat in'. But it's Saturday and after one when I get there, and the place is heaving.

But I'm hungry, so queue for ages and then walk out with it all in one of their paper bags, Cheery Chippy all down the side. Think I'll go back to the gallery and sit on one of the benches near the flower beds – and when I go back inside that idiot couple will have gone. Fancy standing right in front of the canvas, not standing back to appreciate it!

And I'd nearly forgotten yesterday. Yesterday when he said he was letting us loose to express ourselves – paint whatever comes into your mind he said – don't let yourself think about it – just pick up a brush and paint – don't draw anything – just let yourself flow with the colour … and when I realised he was standing just by my left shoulder and lifting his eyebrows and smiling, I couldn't think what to say. Just stood looking at the bright yellows and oranges all mixed together with the blobs of scarlet. And he said – he said – he said, 'Well done, you have really let yourself go.' So perhaps it was OK; felt a bit silly when I looked at the others and you could tell what they had been thinking about. Mine just looked like an explosion, as if someone had dropped a few cans of paint.

So, there I was, sitting on the bench on the right hand side, a bit left of the fountain, and nearly finished the burger and crumbling a bit of the roll to throw to some sparrows having a dust bath near the rose bushes … so easy to imagine we were sitting together by a fountain … that sound of splashing water cooling the air … and a peacock strolls by with that haughty look … and he slides his arm along the back of the bench as I take the last sip of Coke … no, not Coke … I'm just raising the wine glass to my lips … when I see him! Actually walking towards me!

But he doesn't see me; isn't looking my way as I drop the Coke bottle behind the bench and let my hair fall forward. Peering through, I watch him strolling along, arm over the shoulders of Batty Bertram. Of all people, Batty Bertram! She drives us all round the bend when she starts reciting poetry in that soppy voice, soppy or all Dramahatic. New English teacher so we suffer at the lower end of school.

Can't believe he has his arm round her shoulders - and as I watch she leans her head back, looking up at him and he drops a kiss on her forehead and pulls her a bit closer. And they are walking up the steps. She's wearing a tight sort of clinging top and her shoulders are bare, so their skin is touching where his arm rests. And the back of my neck can feel him too. And she is sliding her arm up behind him, slides her hand into the back pocket of his jeans. Can tell she's done that before.

She's all over him; bet she's using that silly affected voice. Why is he so stupid to want to listen to her? I'm hot and cold and feeling a bit sick as I watch them walk through the wide-open doors. And disappear.

And I screw up the last of the burger and chips in the Cheery Chippy bag and chuck it after the Coke bottle behind the bench. And I get up. And I walk across and up the steps; only this time I don't feel happy and excited and walking tall. Feel small and sick. And angry. Why Batty Bertram?

They are not in the first room, nor the second. Can't see them at all. Realise they have not come for the exhibition. So, I go back out into the main entrance hall, there is a corridor leading left and a flight of stairs curving up and round and I see they are up there, just going through a door to the right. And when I go up, I find a sign – Café.

Pretending to read the lists of drinks etc by the door, I can see through to where they are queueing at a counter, heads together. At least he has moved his arm so he can hold a tray and she has taken her hand out of his pocket, and it isn't long before they have moved over to a table by the window. I feel enormous, think my feet are loud on the floor but they don't look up. I don't exist. And I'm at the counter. Ask for a Coke, pass over some money. The boy with the spiky hair grins, nods and says, 'Thank you.' And if I sit over there, I can watch them from behind that big plant thing in the tall pot, and when they leave, they will walk away from my corner.

It's the longest slowest Coke I've ever had. Try to take my eyes away but can't stop watching them, heads together, laughing together, murmuring softly, his hand over hers on the table. I pick up the menu as if I'm thinking of having something else. Blink, try to blink the tears away. See the boy with the spiky hair clear some plates and glasses from two tables. Goes back to wipe them down. Looks over towards my corner so I quickly turn the menu over. And put it down.

He gets up, walks over to the door marked Toilets. She stretches back at the table, stands up, she walks close to the window. It's like a French door and it's open, and she half steps out, lifting her face to the sun. If I were behind her … a quick push … could say I was looking at view … tried to catch her but was just that bit too slow … make a move to stand up …

And he is coming back out of Toilet door, and she is turning to smile – that soppy sickly smile – and he stands in front of her, touches her hair, murmurs something which makes her giggle. The slow torture ends when they walk out. And I look at the half bottle of Coke. Shame to waste it but am not thirsty. I'll never be hungry or thirsty again.

And the boy with the spiky hair pauses by my table, grins and nods his head towards the door. 'Got to hand it to him,' he says.

'?' I look at him.

'Different bird every week,' he says.

'Oh,' I say.

'Yeah, different woman every week. And only a coffee. Every time, only a coffee. Bit tight fisted you know. And you? Are you here for the exhibition? I've not had time, but they say it's good … but I don't know … I don't know much about pictures … only work here at weekends.'

And I hear myself say it's very good and I could tell him a bit about some of the pictures. And he says he finishes in half an hour. He will bring me another drink – on the house. He winks. And I wink back.

IT LOOKED RATHER THREADBARE

Student days and student life − ah! How we remember them − so full of novelty and excitement, discovery and recognition, friendship − and love.

Love − oh yes, we fell in love at the drop of a hat and out of it again. Hearts were broken overnight but mended just as quickly. For I think we all really recognised in that first year it was the sheer headiness of escaping the adoring but restraining parental clutches. After all, our parents could never have felt life as intensely as we did − they had never met such bewitching adorable others − they had never moved into such stimulating worlds.

As I said, that first year was one whirl of emotional intoxication.

After that, of course, life recovered some of its equilibrium and we settled into more mature ways. Not staid stability naturally but we could view the freshers' mad ways with condescending approval. After all, we had been there, done that. And had moved on to − the first few serious committed relationships. First one friend, then another, found their true love and were seen as couples – they were - a couple! – at parties and events.

By the end of that second year there were even conversations about Where We Are Going; when there would be solemn plans for committing to a period Helping in the Third World, followed by world changing careers promoted by Experience ... and so on and so on. I wouldn't have said I was bored but did think when you'd heard one, you'd heard them all.

From which you will gather I hadn't reached the Committed Stage. And I had no plans to do so. Life was still attractively full of a well-chosen course with inspiring tutors, supported by a range of good friends (committed couples and singles). Life could not be better.

So, I was totally unprepared for Peter. Peter blew into my life in a scarlet sports car early one morning in my third year. To be precise it was more a case of I blew into his. The wind caught me suddenly off balance on the Union corner making me step off the kerb clutching at a file of papers. There was a flash of scarlet, screech of brakes and I was sitting on the tarmac. Still clutching the file. But empty - as a swirl of A4 fluttered about me.

And that was that. Peter was embarrassingly good looking in a dark sultry way – a hint of Elvis Presley (who was yet to burst on the scene). And the most charming attentive manners. It seemed only seconds before I was in the front seat, file of papers on knees and being whisked off for a recovering drink.

And that was Peter. And us. We were a couple before I realised. And before I realised it, we were accepted as a couple. We went everywhere together, were invited everywhere together and at every available moment he would roar up to rush me off for a meal at another eating place he had found, a view down the coast he had discovered. And so it went on. Peter had been about during my first year but had a different circle of friends and our paths had not crossed. He had spent his second year in France – 'we must pop over soon, must show you …' and now he was back. Thanking his lucky stars, he had raced round the corner at the right moment.

Within a couple of weeks, he took me home to meet his parents. Thank goodness we went down for the day. A weekend would have rendered me tongue tied and speechless. It just wasn't the sort of life I was used to. Not quite stately home but nevertheless a palatial pile. I was made very welcome – there was almost a sense of relief about his mother – and it wasn't long before it was established my parents were teachers – professional – after which we got on swimmingly.

I was told to come again, soon. But it was a relief when Peter said we must be going.

The rest of the year continued its headlong pace during which it was quite remarkable that we both managed to concentrate on any work at all. A few times I did feel surprised. Social life was increasingly quiet as the year progressed and it became more a leisurely evening with a group of friends than a whiz from one party to another. And several times we spent a weekend with his parents (separate rooms of course) – I had calmed down by now and felt more relaxed in their company. We had rushed up north to see my parents – again a fleeting overnight visit – and Peter seemed to enjoy himself and certainly impressed the folks.

One weekend in May Peter proposed, producing an amazingly large ring. There were congratulations all round and a great party with friends. I did overhear the remark '…thought he'd never settle down …' but chose to ignore it. Although it was surprising to overhear his mother make a similar comment – we popped over for lunch to break the news – along the lines that she had wondered if he would settle down with the right person.

And hey ho, it was on to wedding plans for the following Spring.

So far so good, I hear you say. Not much of a story. The perfect romance.

And it was. Peter was amazing in every way. Just once or twice it crossed my mind that he made the decisions more – but as I agreed with them – was that a problem? Did it matter that he found reasons not to come with me to Vanessa's wedding – an old school friend I hadn't seen for so long and who, if truth be told, had become a rather dull social worker. And that several times we left parties early because he wanted to 'go on somewhere else.' Overall, it was all too good to be true but true it was, and I was delightfully happy. Initially, I had been a bit uncomfortable at the announcement that we would travel after the wedding - I discovered that travel meant travel with no decision on when we should return home and settle down. 'Time enough for that' was clearly meant to reassure but not exactly the route I'd expected my life to take. And as yet he – or rather we – hadn't decided where exactly we would be living.

But, before any of that, Peter picked me up one evening, beaming all over his face and after hugging me tightly, produced a couple of airline tickets from a pocket (you had paper tickets in sweet blue folders in those days). He had booked us a long weekend in Paris. He must show me Paris now!

He was a constant surprise; it was very exciting, but I thought I was gradually adjusting. Fortunately he'd insisted I get a passport ages ago –'You never know when you'll need it' – and so all I had to do was be ready packed the next morning and we'd be off. And he was off, to arrange a few things.

I packed in a bit of a whirl – would I pack the right things? – this? Or that? Or the other? My wardrobe wasn't all that extensive so it wasn't the trial it could have been. Had to settle with what I had – and anyway, he loved me in anything and everything – he told me so often enough. But it was enough to wake me a few times in the night with the result that I overslept.

Peter's knocking woke me and there was a rush around as he laughed. Slamming the case shut at last 'Ready!' a hug and a kiss and we were nearly through the door when I remembered.

'Wait!' I called and dashed back to my bed, picked up Mr Brown, tucked him under my arm and was ready.

Silence.

You could have cut it with a knife.

'What are you doing?'

'Take Mr Brown everywhere,' I laughed.

'Not to Paris with us you don't.'

Silence.

'Wait a minute, I'll put him in the case.'

Silence.

'We're not taking that motheaten old thing with us.'

I looked at Mr Brown. Mr Brown looked at me with his button eyes.

He did look rather threadbare. Grannie had made him when I was a baby and for twenty-two years he had gone everywhere with me. Had held my hand after I had my tonsils out. Had even sat through O levels and A levels without complaining.

I took my coat off.

'What on earth?'

'I take Mr Brown everywhere – he stayed with me in hospital when I had my tonsils out when I was four. I wasn't scared with him there. And I've had him all my life.'

'Not everywhere – you didn't take it when we stayed with my folks. It'll be here when we get back.'

I sat down. 'He was there - in my suitcase; he goes everywhere with me.'

We didn't go to Paris. And Peter was still mystified when I returned his ring. Strangely, neither of us was heartbroken.

BUT THEY GOT THERE

They first met in primary school – Aloysius was two years older and so two classes ahead in school hierarchy, which meant he was well placed to stop Bertie Briggs from gobbing his stale chewing gum into Martha's long curls. The fact that Bertie Briggs promptly swallowed the chewing gum bothered no one, least of all Bertie himself. Being squashed by Aloysius was par for the course in Weatherstone Primary where he, Aloysius and a couple of his mates, delighted in frustrating the ulterior motives of 'the lesser fry'. It did mean that the majority of the school population led cheerful days largely unfettered by the evil intentions of such as Bertie and the three top Juniors enjoyed much appreciated perks from grateful teachers whose play time duties were largely trouble free.

As for Martha herself, not having been aware of Bertie lurking close by working up enough spit to project the gum, she continued on in blissful ignorance of Aloysius' intervention although, like many of her peers, she was very aware of their kindly policing.

And so … on into secondary school … where eventually Martha followed Aloysius … waiting with a few others for the bus at the end of the village High Street and travelling the ten miles over to Middlestone market town. Middlestone High was much larger than Weatherstone Primary of course and the two were even less aware of each other. That is, until Aloysius' final year when one chilly spring evening he missed the bus home after messing about with a couple of mates. He arrived at the bus stop at the same time as Martha – just in time to see the back of the bus disappearing round the corner of the marketplace.

Aloysius looked down at Martha and smiled at her look of consternation and disappointment. Of course, he remembered her but suddenly was aware how her curls framed her face, how expressively her mouth screwed up into a silent Aaargh and how much he wanted to cheer her up.

'An hour to wait,' he said. 'Fancy a milk shake? Or a hot chocolate?'

'Hot chocolate,' and her delighted smile as she accepted made him feel ten feet tall. And that's when and where it all began. Sitting close together in Dolly's Diner in a little booth by the window, sipping hot chocolate and watching people pass by on a chilly spring evening. At sixteen Aloysius had had a few 'dates' – inverted commas because the dates had not even produced more than a couple of brief lip brushes and a vague feeling of 'is that what it's all about?'

But this was different. Aloysius and Martha talked. Talked and laughed. Talked and giggled – well, Martha giggled, Aloysius would have said he chuckled. What about? I have no more idea than they did. The hour passed and the bus rounded the war memorial and parked in the square for the usual fifteen minutes. They left Dolly's Diner and by the time they were seated, they were holding hands. They talked and he held her hand in his all the way back to Weatherstone, where he walked her as far as her garden gate when she agreed to another hot chocolate at Dolly's Diner after school the following day.

The pattern was set. Aloysius and Martha were an item. They were boyfriend and girlfriend. Their friends noted and accepted. Their parents were very soon aware and as time went on, thought it would all die a death. As these things often did. Until the bombshell dropped. Aloysius and Martha wanted to be engaged. At the ripe old age of eighteen and sixteen respectively.

Martha's parents did not refer to Aloysius' grandfather's doubtful business dealings more than once month. And Aloysius' parents only occasionally mentioned the fact that Martha's father was a far too regular habitue of The Dog and Duck. Aloysius' father's reputation with the girls in days gone by was an unfair comment – as were the references to Martha's mother's having been suspected of being very friendly with the milkman. There were many hopes expressed that 'they would grow out of it … come to her senses … could do better for himself …'

And so, the gentle romance ran into the buffers. And the more parents cautioned patience … and time … the more Aloysius and Martha yearned – yes, yearned for each other. It would be no exaggeration to say they pined; pined for each other at each and every separation. Aloysius bought a ring. They declared they were engaged. Of course, the parents could not prevent that. There were some bitter moments – Aloysius was older, he should be exercising more restraint. Martha was in too much of a hurry. They both were. They had not sampled life – which led to some strong words before the air was cleared and it was accepted that Aloysius' father had not actually Meant he was advocating Sampling Life – at least, not in that way. Martha's parents were somewhat mollified that they were all after all singing from the same hymn sheet.

And so it went on. Their relaxed happy relationship was often sadly stretched and emotions very strained. The engagement was On – it could not be Off. But if referred to in conversation at home, always produced some negative response in one way or another. Both sets of parents were in complete agreement.

In spite of each and every date or outing or event being marked by some suspicious or derogatory comment the two lovers managed to maintain a sense of humour and quiet determination. They smiled sweetly and patiently when questioned and checked … in fact, throughout all the furore it was almost unnoticed that Aloysius was making his way through his apprenticeship before qualifying as both electrician and plumber while Martha, after training, became a classroom assistant back in Weatherstone Primary.

And Time moved on. As it does.

Faced with the two young people both now earning and with a future before them, the parents gave way – not very graciously. There was a wedding. And a good face was put on by all those at such a public event, but Atmosphere had been created, Divisions had been sown, relatives having been drawn into one camp or another - or had placed themselves outside the conflict completely.   Not quite true actually. In the case of the young couple – they did not Put on a Good Face – disregarding all that had gone before, they just delighted in what they regarded as their good fortune. They quite simply adored each other and lived for every moment together. Common sense, which both had in abundance, dictated that yes, they had to work but that only enhanced their commitment and complete accord. They threw themselves into their work – but even more so into their relationship.

As could almost be expected, Aloysius proved to be quietly successful and after a while they moved to Middlestone, where he established his own small business, employing at first one and then two apprentices. Martha, after a brief spell at a primary school in Middlestone, resigned to devote herself to first Thomas and then Penelope (generally known as Tom and Penny). Family back in Weatherstone were visited – and visited. But increasingly the gap widened, and the sour atmosphere never completely cleared – almost by now as a habit or established tradition.

The smallest comment – Penny having a health problem ('not from our side of the family!') and Tom failing the 11+ ('takes after their side') were typical indications of ongoing resentment. Aloysius and Martha's transparent happiness was ignored - as was their completely successful marriage. Some friends moved far away. A few relationships failed completely. And more than one was known to be living openly as partners without even a ring for show. But the Aloyisius and Martha frigate sailed calmly through the choppy waters surrounding it.

However, as we said Time moves on.

Penny's health gradually improved and the nightmarish asthma attacks became a thing of the past and the close-knit family rejoiced when life was no longer so limiting.

One could be forgiven for thinking that Tom's death – a horrible accident near the centre of Middlestone when a lorry's brakes failed descending the steep hill and Tom, wearing his new Walkman, failed to hear the driver's frantic efforts on the horn, stepping out from behind a stationary car at the very last moment - would have brought the extended family closer together. But the ghastly scene, so near the school gates and shops, involved many bystanders which made for some continued local reporting, when far too many criticisms and unfounded speculations were made.

Aloysius and Martha drew their consolation from Penny and wonderful memories of the boy they had lost. The three of them grew closer together – if that were possible

– and they refused to respond to any of the comments about how birthday money from grandparents had enabled Tom to purchase the gadget. They did not make any comment on who had given – or not – advice to Tom about precautions he should take.

Sometimes Life seems to drag its feet. But move on it does.

Aloysius' small business prospered although he preferred stability to over expansion – for which Martha was profoundly grateful. It ensured they still had time together and that was their greatest delight. Penny had been quite successful at school and was popular among her peers. They began to quietly anticipate the day when she too would emulate their life and they could enjoy grandchildren.

The fact that it came earlier – so much earlier than expected - was somewhat of a shock. The greatest shock was discovering that Penny had quietly developed a drinking problem as she pursued a relationship with a married man. Penny in love with a boyfriend her own age would have reminded them of their own romance, they could have been sympathetic. Penny slurring her words as she ranted and raved at her abandonment – lover having moved town with his wife – was so much harder to deal with. And made harder by the fact that Penny made sure that everyone she knew – and anyone who was drinking in the Jolly Joker the night she discovered her desertion – knew the lurid details.

All of which proved to the grandparents they had been right all along. No good could have come of it. They had said so repeatedly.

Aloysius and Martha hugged long and hard. She put the kettle on. He lifted the biscuit tin off the shelf. And they sat down at the kitchen table as they had done so often before. And as Penny snored on the sofa, they made a list.

If I told you that on the following day, they sat with Penny and gave her a choice. Have the baby adopted or help us choose the colours as we decorate Tom's old room into a nursery. Agree to complete the nursing course you began in exchange for free childcare from Martha and that Penny agreed, it would all sound so simple and easy and straightforward. She did and they did but it wasn't.

Penny agreed. Her parents supported her. But it wasn't easy. Penny had regrets and resentments, many of which she voiced long and loud in the early days. Martha's knees protested more as time went on and her patience with small children was not as it had been. And Aloysius found the extra expenses sadly coincided with the economic downturn and locating willing apprentices was not so easy.

But they got there!

And by the time Young Tom had his first day at Weatherstone Primary his mother was a fully qualified nurse, his grandmother was bursting with pride as she waved him goodbye at the school gate and his grandfather smiled as he envisioned 'Smith and Grandson' …

SLOWLY AND CAUTIOUSLY

Greg was very caring. He reminded me of this quite often.

Looking back, I remember it was one of the first things I noticed and liked about him. We met when I was quite young and first started chatting when he used to come in the shop where I worked. If it were busy, he'd just buy his usual paper and give me a smile as he paid. But if it were quiet, he would linger and chat a bit. The chats got longer and more frequent and I found that I was looking forward to him coming in. It took quite a long time for him to ask me if I 'd like to meet for a coffee at the nearby cafe after I finished work. And it took even longer before he asked me to go to the cinema with him. We had sat for hours over coffees and tea and toasted teacakes and more coffee. Then it became week by week in fact.

As I said, he was very caring and very interested in me – and that was a nice surprise. I was one of those ordinary nondescript girls. There was nothing special about me at all. I used to look in the mirror sometimes and wish there was just something … better. Wished my hair would curl … or that my eyes were blue not just ordinary brown … or that they were bigger … wished I were taller … or had longer legs … I was just very dull and ordinary. Nobody ever noticed me. I had friends at school … but never got chosen first for anything and somehow none of them ever asked me to join them on a Saturday morning when they were going to meet up in town.

So, you can understand how surprised and flattered I was when Greg used to find time to talk with me and then asked me to have a coffee with him. It really made me aware how very lonely I had been.

My father had died when I was small, and my mother used to say how she had devoted herself to me and had never had time for friends. So, we were very close and needed no one else. And then, she died after picking up a virus and I was left alone. I had to move to a smaller cheaper flat but managed very well on my own.

But Greg changed all that. The coffee out - grew to a film - to a drive in his car to the coast and walks by the sea and after some time he suggested he cook a meal for us at his home. Like me, he didn't have many friends – said he worked hard and hadn't had much time to make new friends after moving to Taunton three years previously.

And then he said … he said … in fact he had been very content on his own until he met me. It made me feel all warm inside and we smiled at each other and raised our glasses. I hadn't drunk wine before … Mum and me couldn't afford much and I had had to budget even more carefully after she died. Now I had wine with every meal with Greg, although we never drank too much. As I said, he was very caring and would drive me home afterwards and wait until I had unlocked the door before driving off. I was so happy then.

It was a wonderful summer.

And when he kissed me for the first time, it felt just right, and I found I was holding him closely. He went very quiet but after a while began to tell me how he felt. Said he was very conscious of the difference in our ages – ten years was a big gap, he said. I shook my head; said I hadn't thought about it at all. And he smiled at me, kissed me again.

A few days later Greg suggested I move in with him. Again, he said he was conscious of the age difference and didn't want me to make a hasty decision. I could hardly believe it. We agreed I would move in, keep my rented flat and my job on for the time being. And it was wonderful. Time passed quickly. My job was just the same – except Greg didn't come in anymore – said he'd only been buying his paper there as an excuse to see me! So, I worked as before but went home every evening with Greg – he would pick me up by the bus station on his way home. He worked in an office – said it paid well but was on the boring side and that most of the time he was on his own. Said that meant he didn't have to spend time in idle chat with colleagues. In fact, he never mentioned any friends. But none of that mattered, we were so close and happy.

When he came home one day, he said he had a surprise for me, we were going away for a few days holiday. He had rented a cottage up on Exmoor – it was old but very well maintained and had a wonderful garden. It was miles from anywhere and we had a wonderful time walking in the area – never saw anyone for the cottage was at the end of a very long lane. And then relaxed in the garden in the evenings. We took turns cooking – Greg had packed a good supply of groceries.

It was a dream holiday.

It changed my life completely. Shortly after that Greg told me that he had bought the cottage and wanted us to live there – suggested we got married and moved out to the cottage. My head and heart were spinning – could not believe all this was happening to me. Dull little me. He said I could give up my job as well, said he earned enough and would like to really care for me completely. I wrote a letter giving notice to my landlord. The same at work. It was all a rush – we wanted to do it NOW. Greg said we should make the most of the end of the summer. I hadn't much to pack and by the next week we were there. In our dream cottage. It came with basic furniture left by the previous owner, and we moved our bits and pieces over in a hired van. It was a good job it was a small van – the lane was very narrow and for the last two miles was only really a cart track.

To be honest I had wondered if we were being sensible, living so far out but Greg explained that he could work from home – by some miracle the Wi-Fi was very good. We had been able to use it when we were on holiday; Greg had spent quite a bit of time on his computer. I hadn't minded and he had said he would teach me how to use a computer when we had time. It was one of those things I hadn't taken to at school and had never bothered after that. Had no use for it. And I still wasn't interested. Life was full with just the two of us, and once Greg had worked from early morning to early afternoon he would switch off his laptop and we were enough for each other.

And somehow … somehow … we put off planning a date

for the wedding. It was not as if we had to contact many friends and family – in fact, no one knew I had moved. There would be time enough – I only sent Christmas cards to Mum's cousin John and his family and her other cousin Tom and as I'd never met them (they lived in Scotland) …

Well, there was time enough.

It was such a happy time.

We drove over to Exeter once a month to stock up on supplies – it was amazing how much we could pack into the car, and I was seeing a part of Somerset I hadn't known. Autumn blew in with its wonderful colours but chillier weather. By the end of October there were some very frosty mornings and bitterly cold winds so Greg suggested I stay home, spend the morning baking some pies for the freezer and he would do the shopping alone. It was a great idea.

As we went into winter, and we walked less, I began to wish for a change for the first time. But Greg didn't want me to go with him in December - said he would be buying my surprise present and that I didn't need to go as I'd already hinted that I was knitting him an Arran sweater. When I said I fancied a change of scenery he was very hurt, regretted he wasn't enough for me, wondered if I wanted to change my mind about marriage. Of course, I didn't and stayed home.

But something happened. I couldn't quite put my finger on it. Whenever I went for a walk, Greg would be with me. If the weather was better in the mornings, he would walk with me and work in the afternoons. I reminded him that I thought it would be useful if I learned to drive – we had talked about it. But he pointed out it would be better to wait until spring; the lane was often a muddy track - almost impassable in places he said once. We could get a firm out with some hard core in the spring.

It was a long winter, so Greg stocked up with supplies for longer; we managed very well. But I was looking forward to going over to Exeter in the spring – or Taunton or wherever he wanted to shop. Greg said we would go to Exeter again – I would enjoy the trip although he was saddened that I wanted to get away from the house. I said it wasn't getting away, just having a change, seeing something else, seeing other people.

The weather improved and we planned to go over the first Monday in April and had a celebratory meal the night before. Greg cooked beef bourguignon – one of my favourites – and opened a special bottle of wine. I did enjoy the evening and fell asleep quickly.

When I woke it was ten o'clock and he was already downstairs – but then I found he wasn't. There was a note on the table 'Couldn't wake you my darling. So I'm setting off now and look forward to seeing you when I get back, all my love Greg'

Tears of disappointment filled my eyes, trickling down my cheeks as I re read the note. I knew it was my fault. I must have drunk too much wine – I never slept so late. Although I thought I'd only had two glasses.

And this is where my story becomes so difficult to tell. Greg never took me to Exeter – or anywhere else again. We would plan it. But I always overslept. Even when I decided not to have a glass of wine, somehow, I would sleep very deeply, and he couldn't wake me. And when I tried to talk about it and suggest we take a drive over later one day he was very hurt at first, said I didn't want him anymore, didn't enjoy our life together, asked if I wanted to cancel the wedding. After a while I stopped asking. And spring drifted into summer.

He loved me so much and I didn't want to hurt his feelings. But it would have been nice to go away from the house for a day. Don't get me wrong. It was a lovely house, and the garden was a joy. Although … I began to feel a bit trapped. And I felt awful about that because Greg was so happy. When he wasn't working, he would sing and was always smiling and would give me a hug as he made a drink, pull me into his arms as he asked me to look at the squirrels in the garden, would hold me in his arms in the evening as we watched TV or a DVD. And that made me feel even worse.

And before I knew it, we were moving into autumn again. The thought that life would shut down in winter made me feel so much worse. Felt ungrateful and selfish. And I decided that when Greg was next driving over, I would insist I should go. He would have to go early October.

But woke up one morning to find he had gone. Never mentioned it. I just went down to find he had left in the very early hours. Had left me a note saying he thought he would make an early start as the weather was due to change later in the day. And was looking forward to being home for dinner.

The weather did change as the hours passed, so it was a relief to see the car headlights coming down the lane. We unpacked the car in silence as the wind grew stronger and finally closed the door with a struggle. And we had our first argument. And the last.

I pointed out that I needed a change, wanted to go away even if only for a day. He said at first how much that hurt him. I said I thought he was being a bit selfish, not listening to what I would like. He grew angry, said he had given me everything. I should be grateful. Pointed out he had spent all the previous day putting up more shelves for me in the kitchen, that he would finish the job the next day. The argument circled endlessly from how I would like to go away even for one day and how much it hurt his feelings, how he was caring for me, looking after me, doing everything for me. Told me that he loved me and if I loved him, I would be content with him and him alone, as he was content with me. We needed no one else, nothing else. Just each other. Said he knew I would soon realise he was right; we were enough for each other. We would have our meal, open a bottle and he would explain it all again to me.

It just went round and round in a circle.

I was standing by the new shelves, nearly finished, tools ready for the next day.

Slowly and cautiously, I reached over and picked up the hammer as Greg bent to take a bottle from the cupboard.

A WEEKEND

Michael crossed the hotel reception swinging his weekend bag casually from his left hand; the receptionist greeted him with a cheerful smile as he reached for the key, 'Good evening sir, Mrs Fitzwarren said to tell you she's on the terrace.'

'Evening Charles, nice place to be in this weather – but I'll drop my bag off first' and Michael headed for the lift.

Charles watched him go, murmuring to the duty porter beside him, 'Wish they were all like that – nice couple – always cheerful and appreciate good service – never a grumble.' The porter nodded, grunted, rustled his paper but was more interested in the 2.30 at Epsom.

As for Michael, it didn't take long to drop off his bag, have a quick freshen up and head down to the terrace. Lisbeth looked up from her book, as he dropped a kiss on the top of her head, and smiled slowly, 'You're early.'

He grinned back, 'Traffic was good.'

'Evening, Mr Fitzwarren.' The waiter placed his drink at his right hand and raised his eyebrows at Lisbeth, who smiled, 'Yes – OK Maurice – I'll have another please.' He took her empty glass.

Michael and Lisbeth smiled at each other, he raised his glass and smiled again.

'Don't wait,' she said. But he held the gesture, Maurice was already approaching with her drink. Their glasses clinked as their eyes met and again that smile … here again…

It was one of their little rituals, to stretch out everything as long as possible. The hot day had given way to a warm evening as they sat there watching the few people in the pool and the casual movement on the terrace below theirs. They didn't talk much, it had all been said before – it made for a comfortable companionship. But eventually they went in to dinner, lingering over the meal; the same dishes had become another of their first night rituals.

It was nearly ten before they headed to the lift; as the doors opened, he took her hand in his and stepping in, pulled her close as the doors met. Inhaled deeply into her hair, then sighed. Lisbeth chuckled softly. 'I know,' she said, sliding her arms round his waist.

Room 320 was cool, half lit by the lights below on the terrace, the bed turned back.

Still holding each other, clothes dropped one by one on the carpet as they walked into the shower. This showering together washed away the time apart, the travel down, all the hiccups of life, made this the start of a new weekend. And the passion afterwards was heightened by the renewal of the continuation.

Waking in a pool of sunlight, Lisbeth stretched, ran a finger along his profile, smiling as he reached for her, eyes still shut.

They slept again.

Breakfast arrived at nine o'clock and they headed for the market at ten. It was one of those very mixed markets – fresh farm produce, some crafts and a range of antiques plus junk and once an artist doing on the spot caricatures, another time a teenage group showed off their skills with guitars and a set of drums. It was never quite the same each time. They wandered as usual, hand in hand, browsing here and there, aware of each other's interests and always buying some fruit and a small item to mark the occasion. Always small and cheap and innocuous – but it was to mark that weekend. Not that they could ever forget.

Back down near the harbour they had a drink outside the pub on the quayside before going in for lunch. Sitting by the window, they could indulge their love of people-watching, making up improbable backgrounds for the passers-by. In the past they had examined the menu but after a few trials had settled on a favourite and no longer even picked up the menu.

'One day,' Michael said, 'They might have a whole new menu and then what should we do?'

'One day … we'll cross that bridge then,' said Lisbeth firmly and picked up her knife and fork.

The very, very delicious fish and chips could always be forgiven as they were followed by a long walk on the beach, usually walking barefoot at the edge of the breaking waves, sandals in hand. They would walk until, by some unspoken agreement, they turned to retrace their footsteps left high by the receding tide.

The walk led inevitably on to the siesta. It had been a long time since waking and longing had never been far away, now there was time to indulge passion and desire. Michael had once said he yearned for her but had been stopped short by her peals of laughter. She said he sounded like a lovesick teenager in an old melodrama - it wasn't a word for a middle-aged couple, she said. It was now a word to be shared when humour was required – they had each yearned for some odd things over time - it had become one of their in-jokes.

And they shared so many things – interests, ideas, thoughts, hopes. All made so much easier by the discovery of this small place by the sea and as yet unspoiled by tourists.

Going in to dinner, they both scanned the restaurant automatically – it was a fairly small place off the beaten track, but you do bump into acquaintances unexpectedly, but again there was no one they knew. They talked more over dinner, a change from the preceding evening when they had been content just to have arrived and be there. Now talk ranged backwards and forwards covering new events and many old topics; they both took an interest in politics but as they mostly agreed there was nothing much new to share there. In fact, they were in so much agreement over so many things conversation was a gentle flow of exchanges. Never getting heated but never drying up and humour never very far from the surface.

Saturday dinner was when they made an effort to have

a change – and they had worked their way through the menu over time. 'Living dangerously,' Michael once quipped. Over the years they had both had friends or colleagues who had exotic holidays, had adventurous trips to far off places, tried the latest in hot air balloons and potholing, but apart from an agreed intention to climb a mountain – 'Snowdon perhaps – one day' – they made no further plans.

Saturday night drifted most pleasurably into Sunday morning with room service once again and time for a last walk on the beach. This time they lingered in the harbour, watching the small boats rocking gently, a man cleaning down a deck, gulls pattering endlessly across cabin roofs. A shared unspoken wish to postpone the walk, which led to the end.

At last, they set off hand in hand across the wet sand gleaming in the morning sun; Michael picked up a large pebble, threw it lazily into the waves. Lisbeth picked up a shell, a dog whelk, turning it slowly in her free hand. They didn't say much. It had been a perfect weekend, as usual. After an hour they turned back.

A light lunch this time in the harbour pub, a few comments on passers-by. And back to the hotel, collected their bags and checked out. The porter, cheerful after the 2.30 at Epsom results, cheerfully carried their bags to Michael's car and bade them a smiling farewell.

'Safe journey, sir. Hope to see you soon. Ah, Thank you sir.' And raised his hand in farewell.

They drove in silence until they reached the station. Michael parked, retrieved Lisbeth's bag from the boot as she got out and slammed the car door. They hugged briefly.

'See you,' they said.

He drove away, not looking back at her walking into the station entrance.

OH, WHAT A FOOL I WAS

No fool like an old fool. That's what they say, and they are right. Whoever they are.

Yes, I'm a fool and no fool like an old fool.

And there's no going back. One mistake, just one little mistake. That's all it takes, and you're done for. I'm done for. Good and proper.

All this time, all these years of getting away with it, all this time of feeling I've succeeded – knowing I've succeeded where others have failed. And then … just that one little mistake. That's all it takes, one little mistake.

Ten years and it's been hard work, always being aware, always keeping watch. Watch over others, watch over my tongue. Never relaxing my guard, it became almost second nature and then I'd remind myself Take care! It only takes one mistake! And I was careful, I was on my guard, I didn't let myself take risks or a chance. Told myself right at the beginning that I must always be alert to every word, every glance – that I couldn't afford even one mistake.

And I did it - I did - I succeeded. Day by day, slowly but surely, I worked and watched and kept my guard up. And from that one handful of coins, I succeeded – all alone and by determination and hard work. For I couldn't afford to share with anyone else, could not afford to let anyone else in on my secret. It had to be mine and mine alone.

Might not have done it of course without the coins. They gave me the beginning, the start of it all. No. Not quite. The start of it all was seeing my chance and seizing it. But the coins greased the way. I never wondered what happened to the master after that. I took my chance - as every man does who wants to be master of his own fate. And I wanted my fate back in my own hands.

So long ago now. Ten years did I say? Has seemed much more, each year a celebration of my success. Every Easter tide I went to church with the crowds - they celebrating the Easter message of Christ risen again and me? Me celebrating my rise, my rise from the ashes of despair. And I would thank God for my chance to rise again, ask for His help. But only then. The rest of the year was too busy, so much work to be done and always the watching, the guarding, the being careful. For you never know from where your end might come.

And I would drop a handful of coins in the church box, to match the handful of coins … gifted me as you might say. Though some would not. I would not pay back those coins – I'd earned them … more than earned … had earned double fold, triple, nay a thousand fold. So, no I would not pay back even if I could. But I gave the coins as a thanks for the start they gave me.

And what a start it was! Why, with those coins I bought the first cloths and pack. Carried it all on my back, peddling from market to market. Pedlar, cheapjack, hawker, chapman ... call us what you will. We give a service to those who cannot travel and there's good money to be made if you buy right. I mostly bought cloth, bright gewgaws and trinkets such as lads buy for their maids, sometimes a potion or pills such as the old and stiff hope will aid their malaise … No use sticking to the same goods, you need to change with the times, with the places.

And stick to your own, your own way. That way I made money, money enough for my donkey and once you look to be a success, so you gain entry to better places and opportunities. Door to door is good, but not so for me unless I stayed near the ports where such as me are not so out of the way. Try knocking on doors way out in the country places and they be afraid – afraid of the difference, the unknown. A black face among all the white? No, in country places stick to the markets where your difference is an attraction. Safety in numbers you see. They feel safe in a crowd, coming to stare, point you out to their friends. And daring each other to buy – putting their money into your hand with a cry of fear and bravado.

But I didn't mind – country markets … town markets or door to door … it was all money and the freedom of the road and of my life. It was my life, to do with what I would. And I would be there still, in sun and in rain, frost and snow and my own master – if it were not for that one mistake.

Oh, what a fool I was. Ten years and always careful, always watching out. But a lonely life in many ways. Even in the crowds, a lonely way of life but one I thought worthwhile. And then I met Becky, a servant girl at the inn just outside Bristol. A good place Bristol, enough black faces to be accepted. For I could never risk London. And Becky made it clear she liked me. I had never thought so far, nor hoped. But she made it clear, she fancied me. And more. But could I share my life with another? Could

I take that chance?

It was temptation. What man would not desire a plump wench with curling hair and laughing eyes? What man wants to lie alone in bed? But I knew the penalty the risk I'd take. I steeled myself. Decided no. Alone I was and alone I would stay. I could trust no other, ever.

She came to me in the stable as I tended Toby - my only true friend, if a donkey can be a friend. She came to me with her womanly wiles and tricks, her hand on mine as I brushed down Toby. Her body close to mine, her breath close to my ear as I bent and her arms, oh God, her arms about me and pressing her body close, her lips on mine. I'm only a man after all. And the hay was sweet and fresh, and her body welcomed mine.

It was after, when we lay, half asleep and she talked of quitting the inn, walking the roads with me … it was then I came to my senses. Told her it could not be. I could not. Would not. Ever. And she raged, my, how she raged. That sweet and smiling woman had such anger within … hit at me when she saw her smooth ways would not sway me. Grabbed at my neckerchief … and she saw.

She saw that which is about my neck. I thought perhaps

not, for she said not a word. Acted as though she was angry but might forgive me, said perhaps we would talk again, perhaps I might change my mind. And fool that I was, I believed her and believed I was safe.

And so we parted, with sad but good humour. And fool that I was, I stayed on at the inn. And she, she who had sworn her fondness, her liking for me, came back in the dark of night with two of her friends. And they seized me, tying my hands behind my back.

She had told them I was rich, I had wealth enough to make it worth their while. Why, she had said, I had so much wealth I even carried it round my neck − the greatest necklet she had ever seen. She was but a silly deceitful wench; they were wiser and knew what they saw.

They would not − because they could not − take the silver from around my neck. My master had made sure of that. It was made fast with a stout padlock, and I had not the key.

But no matter, they said. No matter, the reward for an escaped slave is high. Very high for this one, his master must value him highly, see the weight of silver there. And the name

John White property of Colonel Kirke 12 Pall Mall.

And so Toby, my only friend, is carrying me back to London while they ride beside me; the rope from Toby fast in their hands and my hands secured to Toby's saddle.

With thanks.   Reference

Black and British by David Olusoga

Page 93

The number of these notices from the middle of the seventeenth century to the last decades of the eighteenth, suggests that some of the enslaved in Britain were marked out as human property by slave collars. These were usually brass or copper, occasionally silver, and were riveted or padlocked around the neck and could not be removed. Some carried the initials or name of the owner. In 1756 Matthew Dyer, a goldsmith on Duck Lane in Westminster offered collars for sale as well as 'silver padlocks for Blacks or Dogs'...... In 1685 the London Gazette offered a reward for a fifteen-year-old boy named John White who had a silver collar fixed around his neck that bore the coat of arms and the cipher of one Colonel Kirke.

HE STOOD AND WATCHED

Grey light crept across the sky, hesitantly highlighting rooftops and the church spire. I stood and watched. Yet another day for me to face. Being early summer it was not long before the grey light, now pink tinged, lit and warmed the roofs, the buildings, the trees in the park and then the very cobbles of the streets. And long shadows grew – not dark and definite as they would be at midday but still an indication of the strength of the rising sun.

And with the light came Joe, sauntering idly down the side street into the square, where he paused and stretched, belched, went on his way, trailing his aura of stale beer and sweaty sex behind him. Another night with Belle up at The Dirty Duck, I supposed, her husband being good for nothing after midnight, often sleeping in the bar I'd heard said. Not something I'd ever done – or considered for that matter. Though a night with Belle would have been considered if she'd been around back … when…?

A low humming presaged the arrival of the milk float, starting and stopping as it traversed the east side of the square, then turning down Amberly Street. Several doorways now boasted a milk bottle or two, their white gleaming glass reflected in glass door panels. A black cat, keeping close to the walls, trotted past the butcher and the chemist before pausing, then racing purposefully across the square and up the steps of the wool shop. A tip tap indicated it was through the cat flap and was being welcomed by Bertha, who tried not to worry when he was out all night. During the day he generally dozed in the window, comfortably pillowed on samples of wool, where he was an attraction to old ladies and was often pointed out as a distraction to wailing toddlers, bored by shopping. But at night the town was his, his to survey and sample … the mice in the churchyard knew to dread his coming. The rats under the bridge over the river had learnt to avoid him, though he rarely ventured there, disliking the lap lap of the water against the old stone walls. And the old tom cat living with Mr Arbuthnot in the thatched cottage now retreated indoors when the black cat stalked through the wicket gate. A screeching tussle among the lavender bushes had only resulted in a slightly torn ear and aching claws, and he did not relish a repeat performance. So, he would watch from the safety of the book cluttered windowsill as black cat leisurely sniffed his way along the path before spraying long and well against the bay tree pot beside the front door. Mr Arbuthnot, habitually using the side door and gate, thus had no cause to unjustly rebuke his own cat.

Even as black cat was purring over his dish of salmon pâté, Alan Plummer was unlocking the metal grills over the Co-op doorway before hurrying to switch off the alarms. Close on his heels Ben Orway, who hoped his keen timekeeping and eagerness to assist in each and every task would mark him out as worthy of promotion. Alan Plummer, being more concerned with his wife's inability to budget, had other matters on his mind. The Co-op was always the first to open its doors and Crystal was frequently its first customer, being unable to plan ahead, she was usually in need of her first packet of fags for the day, often supplemented with a lager four pack. Another early customer was Jack Quentin about to set off on a distant job and having as usual failed to organise a packed lunch; skilled handyman of sorts he was in demand over a wide area, his battered truck would be seen outside small cottages and in the upmarket executive 'village' thirty miles distant. Emerging from the Co-op, bag of sandwiches and canned drink in hand, he climbed up into his truck and scraped into gear. Passing me, he gave his usual up and down glance, frowning as he always did.

And as usual, I made no response.

A couple of cars entered and left the square as the church clock chimed eight. Silenced from ten in the evening to eight in the morning, to satisfy newcomers, who had not bargained for their nightly slumbers being disturbed by hourly chimes; it was always a delightful sound to older residents who missed the companionable chimes when they had a disturbed night.

Tom Raynor, leashed dog to heel, walked briskly across the square heading for the park where the dog would first squat to ease its aching bowel and then be released to gambol while Tom bagged the 'necessaries'. Then it would chase after the ball Tom threw from the curved gadget he had purchased at the pet shop. Although designed to make his life easier he had lost the receipt, and therefore its name, and was now compelled to refer to it as his dog's gadget – feeling annoyed by his memory lapse, Tom reminded himself every morning in the park to pass by the pet shop and check out its correct nomenclature. The pet shop, being situated at the far end of Bow Lane, was far enough away from his home to make it a special journey and therefore forgotten until the following day.

He was closely followed by Tracy Synon and her rescue border collie. He was not on a leash - or lead. Rescued from a failing farm and unmentionable conditions, Max had an aversion to any form of restraint. To quite a few people's irritation, Max followed happily at Tracy's heels until told he could 'Go by, Max, go by' when he would race freely and joyfully until she whistled, whereupon he would immediately return to sit by her side. Dog owners, who spent hours and many pounds at dog training classes, were incensed at the apparent ease at which Tracy and Max had bonded and at their complete accord. It must be admitted that Tracy derived quite a sizeable satisfaction from watching Tom Raynor's mounting frustration to get his dog back to heel after he had tired of throwing balls – with his gadget which propelled balls much further than he could have thrown, even back in his cricketing days.

Once both dogs were back under control, Tom and Tracy would walk companionably back together; they would pass by me unnoticing - except for the time his dog paused to cock a leg on my leg and was pulled sharply to 'Heel sir!' and they continued on and over to Chanters Lane and out of sight.

Coinciding with their return, several vans entered the square which now resounded with the clatter of stalls being erected, the metal poles rattling and clanging together and on the cobbles. Being a small market of usually no more than a dozen stalls, the disturbance was short-lived; the vans were quickly unloaded, driven away and the unpacking and displaying began. Long ago the market had included livestock and the cackling, lowing and varied animal noises had added to the hubbub; now it was a more sedate affair – clothing (often racks of jeans and sweatshirts), materials (the rolls varying with the seasons), kitchenalia (a word I had heard only recently), garden tools and produce and the like. Not long ago I noted a new smaller striped stall advertising home-made jams and chutneys and such – and I wondered if it would continue to attract customers. I noticed many looked, but few bought.

Wares set out, the stallholders began their casual survey and general chitchat, relaxing before the hoped-for melee.

Half past eight and the square erupted into the school run – if it could be so termed when the majority of those at primary school walked, cycled or scootered. Several teenagers cut through the square to wait for the school bus at the end of Bow Lane. A few younger boys chased each other in a sort of tag, two passed a football between them as they went; unaccompanied girls tended to walk in small huddles I always noticed and always deep in conversation. Not that I could ever discern any words, whereas it was all too easy to hear the clear boys' voices on the morning air. And mothers, the few there were, often pushed a buggy of some sort with bags dangling from the handle for a little shopping on the way back. One or two walked together but for the most part I noticed, they walked alone, children in their first year at school tended to hang on to buggy handle as if reluctant to part with this last contact with home.

The small shop owners now put in an appearance – it was as good as a stage set - as some arrived on foot or by car to unlock and open up while others, descending from 'desirable flats above premises' had a more leisurely air as they opened doors, took a step outside to survey the scene before retiring, clutching a milk bottle. Harriet – Hair4You – and Victor – VegDirect – always took time to chat outside their adjacent shopfronts. They would gaze earnestly at his display of tempting colourful pyramids, baskets of produce and a few pot plants – he was not one for flowers. All of which contrasted sharply with Harriet's tasteful minimal bust of a haughty profiled female and slim silver vase containing one black velvet rose. Of course, at that distance I could not make out any of their conversations and wondered what they found to talk about for so long and so animatedly.

Nine o'clock coincided as always with the vicar walking across to the church, just off the square, and his hands on the creaking side gate was the prompt for the pair of pigeons to leave their niche behind the corner gargoyles and make their floppy flight in my direction. Why his appearance should disturb them I could never understand – or perhaps it was just a nudge in their well-ordered lives. Creaking gate at nine – move over to the market square. Potter about picking up this and that. Midday saw them fly leisurely down to the river and the pet shop where there were always spills in the yard after unloading. Early evening would see them back in the square before retiring early to the base of the church spire.

Meanwhile, of course, I had them with me for some time. It's strange, I've heard them referred to as the rats of the bird world, but I find them strangely soothing. Granted they can make a mess; their droppings are particularly copious but to my mind more than compensated by their soft consoling murmurings. I see them flying in, swooping down, wings outspread to land on the roof slightly above and to my left. From there I hear their companionable exchanges, the patter of their feet on the tiles until first one and then the other, flutter down to land by my feet. Well-used to my presence, they strut busily investigating the largely unseen until some passing person or vehicle startles them into seeking refuge back up on the roof. Once or twice, one has settled on my shoulder – I'm unsure whether it's a compliment to my quiet presence or merely to save a little wing energy (I am, after all, much lower than the roof or gutter).

A quiet pause in the normal day's events. I stand and watch, my days of partaking are long gone. Not that I was ever particularly active – more the observer – prone to reflecting, cogitating, musing on my fellow man. At such times, past incidents come to mind. The market square has always held me in thrall; many the events, the incidental happenings, meetings and farewells … and crime and romance - even in such a small a situation as this. I stand and watch and remember; the most notable change I would venture to suggest, fashions. Fashions in dress and fashion in attitudes – relations – call it what you will. The manner in which we live and converse the one with the other.

And so it is this morning. The few older ladies, baskets and bags to hand, browse along the produce stall – a pound of this and a quarter of that. A couple pick their way along the rolls of bright cottons, feeling the fabrics, consulting small papers, which I take to be a note of measurements. Are they considering a dress? Curtains? Some of the mothers have returned from the school and, buggies jouncing on the cobbles, they stop to make their purchases, exchange banter with a stall holder.

Tom Raynor returns, minus dog, and examines some garden shears; he does not appear able to reach a decision, opens and closes several pairs, shakes his head. Just as Tracy Synon, but with dog, arrives, large linen bag slung over one shoulder and matching linen hat. She too wanders along towards the small tools, raises a hand in surprise, they chat, Tom still holding the shears. Which are then abandoned as they stroll, seemingly aimlessly round the market, dog close to Tracy's heels. The little café on the corner has opened up, the owner places a board outside; I can see the large cup and saucer from here. They pause, confer and ducking heads, enter. The dog lies down to the left of the door. As I said, romance … ?

Time moves faster and slower at different times of the day. Or so it seems.

For the church clock is already chiming midday and the sun is high overhead. The pigeons have strutted here and there, have swooped over to a more desirable spot, fluttered back up on to the roof once or twice and are looking contented with their lot. More than contented, almost as one, they take off, circle once above the stalls and then head towards the river, wings beating in their seemingly casual way.

The market never gets crowded, at best there may be a bustle near to high days and holidays. Today is none of those. So, people have come and gone, purchases made, or not and Tom and Tracy have emerged at last from the small café; the dog rises, stretches and takes up his accustomed position. They leave the square as the local bus disgorges a few passengers from the nearby villages and the market enjoys a slight resurgence. It appears some people use the market frequently enough to meet up with friends or acquaintances. Greetings are exchanged and after brief tours of stalls, a few head for the café, and a few to the pub on the corner. None spare me a second glance; they are so used to my presence. Naturally it was not always so.

Old John Upton, ninety if he's a day, weaves his slow way into the square and dismounts stiffly outside the pub. Removes the clips from his trouser legs after leaning the bicycle against the horse trough, filled with a colourful display of geraniums, and touches his cap courteously to Priscilla Wearing as he passes her and goes into the pub. He will be there for an hour and half.

There is a lull in activities and those about their business seem to proceed with a slower deliberation. Time for stall holders to set off for a drink, bacon sandwich or such from the café or pub … they seem to have evolved an easy camaraderie over the years, watching over stalls or buying for each other.

Only a little later the soporific effect is abruptly disturbed by a faint clamour in the distance. Which is explained by the appearance of a crocodile of children, about nine years old I would hazard a guess, and led by a tall thin young woman with curly hair. She halts at the entrance to the square on my right, casts an eye back, calling out to the queue behind her to remember what she told them.

Silence descends as she marshals them into the square; they tour the square, away from me to the right, pausing every so often and from the raised hands I surmise she is asking questions. I see them every now and then in the gaps between the stalls and then moving along the left of the square, halting by the horse trough. A longer pause there – perhaps she is telling them about the horses who would, in days gone by, slake their thirst.

And finally, they are nearing where I stand and watch. And they stop, forming a semi-circle, looking up at me. The young woman looks them over, waits a few moments and then asks,

'Can anyone see the inscription I told you about? The plaque?'

A number of hands are raised and several wave with sibilant, 'Miss … Miss …'

'James,' she says. 'Can you read it for us?'

A dark-haired boy steps forward and pointing below my feet, reads out,

'To The Memory of Cedric Carter

Merchant of this Town

And who donated much to Charity

And by whose Bequest also Twelve Alms-houses

Benefit Twelve Aged and Needy of this Parish

1710 – 1780 AD

And they all clap.

It is so long, so very long since I heard mention of my name that I forget to listen. But I recover. Miss is telling them something of my life … talks of charity and kindness … asks if anyone can remember why the letters AD … answers a few questions. There are some comments about my hat – my hair – the buckles on my shoes – all the while they stare and point.

Then Miss suggests it is time for Peregrine to have his turn. Peregrine, a fair-haired lad, steps forward and I note he is clutching a bunch of flowers. He clears his throat and announces, 'My Gran said I was to bring these flowers 'cos she lives in one of them alms-houses and she's ever so glad Mr Cedric built 'em.' And the flowers are placed by my feet.

Another round of clapping.

I wish I could respond.

A thin girl with a peevish expression says, 'My Dad let me watch them pull a stachoo down on TV and chuck it in the river. My Dad says all them stachoos should be chucked in the river.'

Miss slowly explains that it might be a good idea to learn about each statue and what each person commemorated did in the past. Peregrine calls out his Gran likes Cedric and what he did, so there.

Miss smiles and says his Gran must have done her research and then places a large bag she has been carrying on the paved area and proceeds to distribute notepads and pencils; the children all squat or sit and begin … well, to draw me! Miss looks more relaxed, takes a deep breath and sits on the flowerbed wall.

There's a scraping of gears as Jack Quintin, draws into the kerb, switches off the engine. He leans out of the cab window, asks if anyone can join the class. Miss, looks amused, nods and smiles. So, Jack Quintin strolls round the group, admires what he refers to as their artwork and then sits beside Miss and proceeds to tell her that he thinks it a shame, a shame that the town has neglected me for so long. Says he has started a Restoration Group and I am to be their first project. Miss and Jack Quentin seem to have a lot to talk about. I try to see the notepads below.

FOR THE LAST TIME

If you had stepped through the door of the Copper Kettle that morning you would have been hard pressed to spot a vacant table as the hum of conversations almost drowned the low background music – the owner's choice of popular 60's. But you didn't, so we don't have to concern ourselves whether or not you fulfilled your desire for a toasted bagel and strong black coffee.

Waitresses Wendy and Tamsin were not exactly rushed off their feet, being well used to busy mornings and had long adjusted to an orderly pace which kept customers happy as they maintained their seemingly relaxed service. Coffees and teas … small cakes and pastries … toasted specials … all were making their way to the right destinations all with welcome pauses, which allowed for conversations to also pause, pick up and progress; either on the same wavelength or follow a digression. And, as usual, both waitresses could see how happy and relaxed their customers were as their needs were anticipated.

In the bay window, with its cheerful flower sprigged

curtains looped back, at a table for four sat only Mary Anderly with her daughter Dinah Dibbs, both with cheerful smiles – which would only have struck you as somewhat fixed if you had been watching them for some time. Mary had booked the table earlier that week, specifically requesting the table in the bay window – it afforded slightly greater privacy. Mary was determined to have a cheerful coffee hour with Dinah but was very much afraid her eyes would fill with tears at some point – if indeed she did not break down completely. But mothers are made of sterner stuff - goodness knows they have had practice as they watch their children pass through the various stages. From wobbly toddlers to apprehensive first school days, from up and down, on and off friendships to teenage romances and then the trials of watching but saying nothing as young marriages struggle through their initial troubles. Mary and her daughter Dinah had had many coffees or teas at the Copper Kettle; more recently they had not been so frequent, so this morning was an especial treat for mother and daughter.

'Another cup?' asked Mary, picking up the teapot, praying inwardly 'Say yes - just one more? Please'. And battening down the inward sigh of relief when Dinah smiled gently, 'Yes please, Mum.' There was a silence as tea was poured, milk added, tea stirred, both looking down and concentrating on their slowly moving spoons.

And then, Mary made a determined effort, 'Like we have kept saying, it's not so far these days what with Skype and Zoom and air travel being what it is. And you are making the right choice – you will have a much better life over there. And I will make the trip out at least once to see how it all is – I can't imagine … and we can keep in touch these days so well - good job we've practised with Zoom – I can still watch the children growing up. No, don't say anything. We've said it all before, lots of times. When you finish that cup of tea, I want you to get up and walk out. Don't look back. And I will sit here for a bit longer, remember the times we have sat here, and you have told me so many special things. So many happy times to remember. And like I said, I don't want to come and see you off – hate goodbyes – this way I can think about meeting again – it's not a goodbye – this isn't for the last time - it's a 'till next time'. '

Peter Donnelly, at the table in the corner left of the bay window, pulled a face, 'Tried to get that table in the window, it's a bit more private. Still, don't suppose it makes much difference'. His wife Jane looked over towards the service door, 'Hope they aren't too long – I'm dying for a coffee.' Peter frowned at the exaggeration and opened his mouth, closed it again. There was no point now. Jane would sail blithely on with her exaggerated pronouncements, her extreme reactions, her waves of enthusiasms – none of it would irritate him anymore. For years they had struggled without recognising it as such, thinking married life was perhaps meant to be like this, after all they were two different people and were bound to feel differently about things. Weren't they?

He was glad they had never had time to consider starting a family – they had both had interesting careers and their greatest bond had actually been their willingness to lead quite separate lives at times. They had both, in turn, been required to travel for long periods and it was perhaps their separations which had helped to keep their marriage afloat.

They were meeting now to discuss the final details in their separation – the final separation. By now they were both living in different towns, had agreed to return and spend a last night packing a few items, checking any paperwork (hopefully by now minimal). It had gone quite amicably, meeting at the house, she had ordered a takeaway and the few final ends were tied and knotted and filed away for ever. Their solicitor had been reluctant initially to handle their case together, could not believe that there would not be some last-minute recriminations. Much to his surprise, all had gone smoothly, and he would be handling the sale of the house from tomorrow.

The coffees arrived and two small pastries on a white plate. Their favourite Portuguese custard tarts. Jane lifted her cup, smiled and said, 'For the last time.'

Peter smiled back, 'For the last time.'

Watching them raise their coffee cups in a toast smiling at each other, Freddie thought bitterly, that could have been us in twenty years' time if only … he looked back at Tina's bent head, the fingers of her right hand absently twisting and turning a strand of the long red hair he loved so much. Her left cheek was resting on her hand, and she was looking down at the slice of coffee and walnut cake as if she had never seen one before. Holding back a sigh, he tried again.

'If there's nothing actually wrong,' he began. 'If I haven't done anything … why not give yourself more time? Think things over – I'm not trying to rush you. I just want you to be sure you know what you're saying. We've had some good times together, haven't we?'

Tina nodded, leaving her hair to fall forward over her face. Poked the slice of cake with her fork, picked off the walnut and ate it. 'It's not that, Freddie. You haven't done anything wrong. It's just that you want me to be serious … settle down … talk about engagements and getting married … it's not how I feel.'

'In that case,' cut in Freddie quickly. 'I can see I've maybe rushed things … gone too fast for you. I can wait. We can take things more slowly. I forget I'm a bit older – of course, you want to have fun – enjoy being young and not get tied down too soon. I can wait – a year – or two … and then?'

But Tina shook her head, 'It's not that Freddie. We wait a year or two and you say you'll still want to settle down – get into a mortgage and a house and probably a family. And I don't. That's not what I want at all. The world is changing – homes and families – everything just like our parents had – all that isn't going to work. The world is changing – I don't want to be tied to a mortgage and a house – I want to be free to go - oh, anywhere - work round the world and back again. And children – what sort of future can you see for children? The world is changing and everything is going to be so much harder – it already is – and the stability you talk about – it may not last. What kind of a world would we be bringing children into?'

She drank some coffee. Freddie stared, lost for words. But not for long. Began to explain once more, slowly and patiently, how he felt, how he saw their future together, how he was willing to wait, perhaps to travel with her – after all, it could be good experience. By now Tina was chopping her cake into fragments, eating the creamy edges, taking impatient sips of coffee. Suddenly she put down the fork. Put her hand on her bag. Said softly but calmly, 'It's no good going on and on Freddie. For the last time, I can't and won't marry you. I wish you well, but I don't want to ever see you again.' And with that she pushed back her chair and walked quietly out of the cafe.

He made a half-hearted movement, sank back down on his chair. And then poured himself another cup of coffee, stirring it slowly he gazed at her half-eaten slice of cake, pulled the plate towards him, slid the cake over and began to finish it. Funny, he'd never heard her talk that way before. He'd thought they got on very well but if she were thinking that way, perhaps best to find out now and not later.

Paula watched Tina's departure, glanced back and seeing Freddie's downcast face thought she had just missed a lover's tiff. Hoped they'd make it up. In the meantime … In the meantime, she had to change Dave's mind – or try to. Both of them having lost spouses and then meeting and starting a relationship, they had known great happiness, she had believed her life was set sail for peaceful waters. Meeting in their fifties, it had been a surprise to both of them how easily they had drifted into a companionable and contented relationship. For a while they had toyed with the idea of selling up and buying a house together but after some discussion they had agreed to stay with the status quo.

Dave had remarked once that it lent a certain spice to their life – moving between two homes, both so very contrasting. And added that it made him feel quite the lad, having a mistress. Paula, taken aback at first, then roared with laughter and agreed that she might drop the odd bombshell at the Book Club – which consisted mainly of older ladies in pastel blouses – and mention she was 'spending the night with her lover.' Added that she might do it several times but not explain it would be the same chap. It appealed to their sense of humour.

And so it continued. And might have continued that way – a week in Paula's very untidy cottage, overflowing with what she termed her 'stuff', having no better description for the weird and odd collection of things she used in her still life paintings and then a couple of nights at Dave's neat well organised expensive flat, which was so very convenient for the theatre. They had never had a set routine. Time here, time there. Longer or shorter. And then the holidays away together. Retirement had far exceeded their expectations.

It was no reflection on their earlier relationships – they had had perfectly happy marriages, both of them. But it was so far in the past that it seemed like a favourite book or film, remembered occasionally with deep affection. Their friends and families had long accepted the seemingly casual situation, life had moved on in its seemingly perfect and comfortable way.

Only now, Dave had dropped his bombshell the previous week and they had reached stalemate. In a nutshell – if only it could be packed into a nutshell, thought Paula despairingly, and buried away somewhere. Some time ago Dave had been diagnosed with a terminal illness – they had reeled, pulled themselves together, listened to consultations, adjusted their lifestyle and carried on. After all, they had each other and that was all that mattered – ignoring the final end of their story, pretending, without saying, that what was ignored could be ignored.

But now, the final stage had sneaked in upon them. And Dave, having made his decisions and preparations earlier, now announced they would be put into practice. Moving into a hospice was inevitable and would have to be sooner rather than later. Much sooner. He explained all to the love of his life, who said she couldn't be if he were to ignore her wishes. But Dave, who had cheerfully learnt to abandon his neat, organised lifestyle and live casually in Paula's cottage, relax in her muddle of books and canvases, potter among the overgrown garden and orchard and equally proudly carry her off to Glyndebourne for a special weekend and who had always appeared to agree with her ideas and suggestions, had suddenly, inexplicably, dug in his heels.

Soon, very soon, he would have to move into the hospice – arrangements were already in motion – and he wanted to draw the line there. Paula was to remember him as he was and had been. The end was to be his alone. The discussion had been brief – after all, a discussion cannot be one sided. They would have this week down at her cottage doing their favourite things – like coffee here at the Copper Kettle for the last time – and she could drive him back to his flat. For the last time.

He was quite calm and matter of fact. Paula had whirled through a range of emotions of such intensity she could hardly think in a reasonable manner, before surfacing to float with him on what seemed to be calm waters. This last week had been filled with simple pleasures and they shared an understanding, giving each other mutual strength. Their cheerful faces, when Wendy carried over a second pot of coffee, gave her an inner glow.

Meanwhile, over by the service door – which had been the only table empty when Frances and Philippa hurried in, laden with bags and bundles – there were no smiles. Wendy had nodded briefly in their direction as she passed Tamsin by the coffee machine, raised her eyebrows, and carried on. It was their usual indication to each other that all was perhaps not well, an eye for service had better be answered promptly. So, although the two friends had hurried in later than planned, were at the awkward table where movement in and out of the rear kitchen meant conversation could be interrupted, Philippa and Frances were receiving the very best attention.

A turn of the head had a waitress responding as if by magic. In no time at all they had Tea for Two and a plate of scones, bowl of cream and pot of homemade strawberry jam with all the accoutrements laid before them. And yet, not a smile. The conversation was somewhat stilted and formal, teaspoons and small knives received far more attention than usual.

'Shall I pour?' asked Frances, after a moment.

'Please do,' was the polite – nay, frigid response.

Frances poured with careful attention to positioning of cup and saucer, the pouring of a little milk, the angle of teapot spout and finally passing of cup and saucer. She then poured herself a cup of tea with equal attention to detail. Philippa made no comment apart from the conventional 'Thank you.'

Both ladies then placing a finger on the plate of scones attempted to push the plate in the others direction and there were a couple of 'After you's.'

'Not at all, after you.'

After which both seized a scone and savagely sliced it through. Philippa was a cream first and Frances was a jam first so there was no possible conflict in the next procedure as they both knew each other's preferences – and why shouldn't they when they had followed this routine every week for the past … how many years?

The silence continued as both ladies took a sip of tea, delicately patted the lips with a napkin and halved a half scone. Cream followed by jam, jam followed by cream demanded great attention and then careful positioning of small knives.

Small bites were made. And a sip of tea. A dab of the lips.

Back by the coffee machine, Wendy paused, shook her head slightly and carried on.

And then.

'I should have said,' – Frances.

'Yes. You should.'

'I was a bit taken by surprise.'

'I suppose you could have been.'

'I was … and I'm sorry.'

'I suppose you just weren't expecting it.'

'Of course not … but all the same, I'm sorry.'

And two ladies smiled small smiles at each other.

'More tea?' asked Philippa.

'Don't mind if I do,' said Frances.

And that was how the Great Rift was mended. The church flower ladies would have heaved a collective sigh of relief had they been a fly (or flies) on the wall. Not that the Copper Kettle had flies on its walls: the staff were most careful.

And what had brought about this stiff exchange?

Their small local church had been honoured by a surprise visit from the Archbishop (and entourage); there had been much fluttering at the shortness of the notice but all had gone well. The vicar kept his sermon short and to the point, the congregation swelled by family members and friends put on a good show and the pair of pigeons, which usually added to the service, had been diverted by a plentiful supply of grain at the far end of the churchyard. And all would have been well, it would have been a day to remember. Well, it was. But not for all the right reasons. The Archbishop paused as he left the porch and requested the name of the Wonderful Flower Arranger – he had been most impressed by the floral arrangements. By unfortunate coincidence as it happened, Frances had been nearby hoping to take a discreet selfie – just might get his Lordship in the background. Vicar, spotting her, insisted on an introduction.

Frances, mind all intent on a selfie, had murmured a few deprecating comments to the extremely kind and rather lengthy praise. Philippa, also close by (although not intent on a selfie) had hoped – nay, expected - her close and bosom friend to say - perhaps just a few words giving credit to the magnificent blooms she herself had insisted Frances pick from Philippa's own garden.

The Archbishop and entourage had moved on. And departed. Leaving behind a Rift – a Chasm – a Hurt between two close friends.

But we are talking of the Copper Kettle and two old friends.

'A storm in a teacup,' smiled Philippa as she signalled to the ever-ready Wendy. 'Another pot of tea, please.' And both ladies smiled as she hurried over. Not for the last time did a cup of tea works wonders.

In contrast, there had been a celebratory atmosphere at the table in the far corner just left of the fireplace – filled of course in the summer with a tasteful arrangement of fake but very realistic flowers. Emma and Kate, seated with their backs to the wall so that they could watch for their respective mothers, ordered a couple of coffees knowing they were early and could cast an appreciative eye over the cakes and pastries list as they waited.

Kate had reserved the table telling Wendy that it was a

special occasion, knowing that the Copper Kettle liked to make a token gesture. Their table therefore with its larger vase of roses and a bow of ribbon on each corner of the tablecloth had attracted the attention of regulars who knew that some Occasion was afoot, and a few smiles had been directed that way. Not that Kate or Emma had noticed, being totally wrapped up in their conversation and each other.

'For the last time,' said Emma.

'Oh, I don't know. We'll be back … have to come back sometimes.'

'I meant it will be the last time we can do it like this – next time we'll be an old married couple. It'll be different … look, your Mum first as usual.'

And they waved to the plump woman in the doorway gazing round. She waved back, walking over and slipping her jacket off her shoulders as she reached the table, bent over to kiss them both before sitting down with a satisfied sigh.

'All done. All checked. All shipshape and Bristol fashion,' and she leaned back in her chair with another sigh. 'Nothing left to do but sit back and enjoy ourselves.'

Kate's mother had taken charge of the wedding arrangements, persuading Emma's mother that with five daughters she had far more experience and added that this would be her grand finale – 'and if any fail and do it for a second time, they needn't call on me.'

Emma's mother had gladly acquiesced, still (to quote her very words) trying to 'come to terms' with it all. As she had said to her husband every night as they lay awake in bed, 'I've dreamt about it ever since she was a little girl. The village church is so pretty … and I could see you walking her down the aisle … the white dress …and the flowers …' and she would sigh. There would be a pause and then, 'But it's not to be … where did we go wrong? … who could have imagined? … and a registry office! …. Cousin Sybil says she's never heard of such a thing … everyone in our family has always been married at church … and it's so pretty …'

And that was the cue for her husband to put a comforting arm about her, hug her gently. 'We've done nothing wrong – and you must admit they are so very happy – as for the church, there's always a first time for everything.'

So now, when Emma's mother appeared in the doorway, they all three made a fuss of seeing her seated with hugs and a kiss and the menu and a flurry of comments and questions so that the initial minutes had nary a pause in which she might feel uncomfortable. Pots of tea and more coffee and plates of assorted small cakes appeared in record time as both Wendy and Tamsin put best foot forward. Unsure of what the special occasion might be, they smiled warmly at all four as they checked everything was in order, retiring to the coffee machine for a brief speculation before heading off to different tables.

Tamsin to table 4 for the third time. Susie and Jennifer had been there for a long time and were even now ordering their third pot of tea. Jennifer had had recourse to the Ladies, but Susie had sought refuge there four times - more to dab her eyes, bathe them in cold water and once snivel into a tissue before snorting and taking a deep breath than to relieve her bladder. Alone at the table each time, Jennifer had gazed sadly at the pretty flower arrangement in the centre of the table, wonder how much longer she could spare and twice consulted her phone. Susie was back, seated herself and smiling bravely.

Jennifer poured her another cup of tea, raised her eyebrows at the last cake left on the plate. Susie shook her head. There was a silence.

At last Susie took a deep breath, 'I'm sorry Jennifer. I

thought it would be easier than this. You have given me plenty of time to get used to the idea and I truly believed I would handle it better. You have been so good for me; you deserve better than this.'

Jennifer smiled, 'Thank you.'

Another pause. Before Susie tried again.

'I suppose I would have managed – you have to. But you really did help me get through those awful first months when Timmy left me. And I'd never have thought of joining things – never thought that would do any good at all. But you're right – I have made some new friends – and I do have places to go to and things to do. But it all thanks to you – we'd only been here for a few months, and I knew no one else at all.'

'But you did it yourself, I only helped a bit,' said Jennifer. 'Gave you some encouragement.'

Susie laughed, for the first time that morning.

'Encouragement?' she laughed. 'You gave me push after push – and if I didn't move, you dragged me off – first to one thing then another.'

Jennifer opened her mouth in dismay.

By now Susie was giggling – it was as if a dam had burst.

'No – admit it – you were going to make me do things – meet people – get involved – you were always there at first – Susie, can you? – Susie, will you? - Susie, how about? …'

By now Jennifer was smiling – beginning to chuckle. 'Was it that bad?'

'Oh yes, but you were quite right. And I can never thank you enough. I shall miss you – more than I can say. But I'm pleased for you – really I am. I hope you will write or phone and let me know how you both get on, settle down. Roger will enjoy the new job and I bet you will start getting involved in things straight away. Just let me know.'

'It is going to be different – but Scotland is not the back of beyond. Once we are settled down and organised, you must come up for a visit. We'd love to see you; hear how you are getting on. I've checked, there are cheap air tickets – unless you want to sit on a train watching the world go by.'

Susie stared. 'Visit? You mean this is not for the last time? … It'll have to be a plane – I don't watch the world go by anymore.'

And they were both laughing.

James and Olivia, deep in conversation at the next table, paused for a moment, enjoying the sound of the laughter. James' faded blue eyes crinkled at the corners, 'You used to laugh like that. Like bells in the wind.'

'Get away with you,' returned his wife. 'You are a sentimental old fool, James. Bells in the wind indeed. Whatever next?'

And wished she hadn't.

For her husband went into one of his serious moods and she was not disposed to be serious. She wanted to enjoy sitting at a table with a pretty posy of flowers and delicious little cakes, which she had not had to make but which tasted just as good.

'What next? I'll tell you what next. This is the kind of thing we shall miss and not be able to do easily. Before I forget, remind me to put this on the list.'

'Put what on the list?'

'The Copper Kettle. Get that list out of your handbag and add Copper Kettle. It's no good Pammy saying Make a list Mum and I'll always get it for you, if we don't use it. Go on, get it out now while I find my pen.'

And James began to dip into his jacket pocket where he always kept a pen and a couple of dog biscuits for whenever they met a dog. Olivia meanwhile rummaged in her capacious handbag and found The List, which was on the first page of the new red Notebook. The new red Notebook which was part of the Helping You Move. Daughter Pammy was the organising kind and meant well. The Notebook was another of her ideas – if her parents would write down their thoughts, wishes, ideas, needs, whatever … it would all help towards helping them adjust to the changes about to happen.

It was she who had dropped them off that morning and would pick them up again at eleven thirty. It was Pammy who had organised visits to Sheltered Accommodation and various Homes and Alternative Lifestyles. It had taken some time for James and Olivia to accept that they were not coping easily in their large house and garden, that hired help was not really the answer, that unexpected accidents had shown how vulnerable they could be. It had been a slow process.

And the process had reached the stage of house and contents up for sale as from the next Monday – apart from the essential and sentimental items which were at that very moment being moved into the convenient flat in a retirement complex all three had agreed upon. And where Pammy would take them at eleven thirty.

'We are not here for the last time,' declared James firmly. 'Write down Copper Kettle on the first Saturday of the month. And we shall always have something to look forward to. Now, have we time for another cup of tea?'

There was a bit of a lull, the murmur of conversations faded momentarily then revived. There was a stir as a couple left … a settling of bills … a gathering of bags and jackets … the morning rush was ebbing. Twelve to twelve thirty was always a quiet time. As Wendy and Tamsin drank a welcome coffee, they agreed dealing with so many happy customers was what made the job so enjoyable.

YOU HAVE UNTIL 30th APRIL

Five pens scribbled – a couple quickly, confidently, two were slower and one hesitated halfway. Five pads and notebooks were closed and stowed away in bags.

And so, the latest Writers Wrangle closed promptly at twelve thirty.

It had been, as usual, a most enjoyable morning. Five offerings had been deposited on the altar of Progress and found satisfactory; one indeed had merited longer scrutiny even as it was agreed to be Worthy of 'doing something with it'. Such commendations were, while not rare, certainly not frequent. Suitably thrilled but also with a modest air, the recipient smiled with downcast eyes and a deprecating wave of the hand - Priscilla knew better than to beam with delight.

It just didn't do to appear as though any praise was well deserved – no matter how one felt it jolly well was. Each and every member of the Writers (for as such they privately termed themselves) was well versed in the art of seemingly artless surprise when praise was forthcoming. As praise and recognition were the Writers watchwords, there was a good deal of quiet smiling, and casual hand gesturing. And if there were any small yearning for an outburst of very high praise, a universal outpouring of admiration, it was kept well under wraps.

And so it was that twelve thirty saw the departure of four Writers with much handwaving and thanks for yet another amicable get together, and a reminder that they had until the thirtieth of April when they would meet at Priscilla's. The fifth Writer, smiling vaguely, wondered how quickly she could clear the scattered china, restore cushions to their usual self-satisfied plumpness and tidy away a few reference books (one offering had resulted in some mild disagreements on geographical possibilities) before her beloved but stickler-for-tidiness husband appeared for his lunch.

Daphne enjoyed hosting the Writers Wrangle, it gave her an opportunity to show off her cake baking skills. Not once had she repeated her coffee and cakes menu but sadly, she had realised that her continued originality had passed by completely unnoticed. Yes, the cake of the day would be pronounced Delicious which was almost enough for Daphne – but was it too much to ask that someone, anyone, would one day say wide-eyed, 'Gosh, it's yet another Different Cake! '

A last wave and smile and she closed the door, began a rapid gathering up of cups, crumbed plates, dropped teaspoons as she headed for the kitchen. A nutritious and tasty cold combination of meats and salads was retrieved from the fridge, its covering removed as it was placed on a tray already set with cutlery, plates, and glasses. Edgar was also a stickler for punctuality, and she glanced at her watch as she hastily thumped and reset cushions, grabbed a couple of books to stuff back in the bookcase. And there was the sound of car wheels on the gravel outside. She lifted the water jug from the fridge as the front door opened.

If only … passed through her mind.

Driving down the country lane, windows down, Classic Radio louder than usual, Priscilla thought One of them, just one of them, could have been really, really enthusiastic! But oh no, … very enjoyable … I read it again … I did like it − DID − ha! … if they thought it was good − Good! − why couldn't just one of them put a finger on what really succeeded? Suppose I came off better than Marigold − no one said very much about her story. But then, what could you say? It was much the same as usual. All the old phrases and platitudes, am I the only one to think that all her stories have a sameness about them? Nice, yes. They have a plot, a theme, the descriptions … they all take place in nice places, to nice people … and the endings are always so neat. They are nice and comfortable. All so very predictable.

Overtaking a cyclist, a little too closely, she slowed briefly to circumnavigate a sauntering local leading a placid fat pony, before regaining her speed and line of thought.

Or am I wrong? Am I mistaken? Perhaps it's me who is … well, not nice and kind – after all, I'm only mildly good, a good read. Is that what I want to be? To be a Good read? Thought I really had written something better this time, thought I'd Said Something … something that would make them sound excited. That I'd said something that would have them going.

If only … passed through her mind as she put her foot down on the crest of the hill.

Deborah, on the other hand, driving with due care and attention along the country lane away from Daphne's, relished the peace and quiet – she could ignore the sound of the engine – away from the voices, the incessant competing for attention. Why did they have to talk all the time? Why couldn't there be quiet moments of reflection

162

after a particular phrase or thought was up for comment?

This was so often the way her mind worked after a Wrangle. So aptly named, she thought, it really was a wrangle at times – more inclined to noisy argument than debate and persuasion. Her mind, inconsequentially, moved from wrangle to wrangler and an image of a relaxed cowboy ambling through the scrub - to wringer. Wrangler … wringer … and she imagined thoughts and ideas, plots and propositions steadily going through her grandmother's wringer to emerge all neatly pressed. It was all so much slower then, she thought. Slow and careful. Kinder too. A bit like Angela.

How on earth could Angela write such … such nice stories? Their very niceness, their pleasantness, meant that she was living in a dream world, did not see the ugly side of things. Her characters might make mistakes, but were never truly evil, never committed acts of such outrage that others were affected for the rest of their lives. To her, poverty meant life was hard, things were difficult, but it was not insurmountable, life could be turned around. Only in real life, that didn't happen, not so easily. For Angela, the most villainous villain either repented or was neatly disposed of with an almost clinical smoothness.

In reality, poverty could twist and turn the mind into actions that hurt, left an indelible stain so that the recipient was never ever again completely free. Life, it is true, moved on, and you with it but a memory would stay, would rise unbidden, change the seemingly carefree now to suddenly, frighteningly, into the past torment. It only took a word, a phrase, to hurl one back.

If only … one could really forget, she thought.

She had the shopping list somewhere. Angela kept her eyes on the endless stream of traffic on the roundabout as her hand scrabbled in her bag – perhaps it was in her pocket? There was a gap, she put her foot down and hurtled into the fray that was midday in the centre of Tuxton. Nothing venture, nothing win she thought as she raised a hand in acknowledgement of an outraged driver compelled to slow down. And resisted the temptation to make it a one or two finger salute. The latter, reversed, she knew was rude but not as rude as the former – not that she was very sure of either.

Nor did she really want to know, like much in life. There was it seemed, two ways of living, one nicer than the other. Angela was tempted to say better but that was more judgemental and that she did not wish to be. No one is infallible she was prone to say, let he who is without sin etc. There were those, of course, who chose to lead … well, more disreputable lives but she liked to think that they didn't really mean it, they were thoughtless and would eventually be restored to a more acceptable way of life. If asked, but no one ever did, Angela would have been compelled to admit that she probably thought that everyone was innately nice, lapses were lapses, but humankind was basically 'nice'. And it would 'all work out'. She could no more believe in a vengeful Almighty than she could believe there were people who were intent on doing down their fellows as a career choice.

Slipping into a parking place outside Tesco, Angela sighed as she retrieved the shopping list from the footwell. What would tempt David, bring a smile of approval?

If only … if only he noticed what he was eating and understood the effort she made.

Marigold had set off home at the same time as the others, halfway round the roundabout she suddenly thought of Martin's comment early that morning. Pulling her back into bed, he had nuzzled the back of her neck, whispering Mrs Dearest Darling must you get up? One thing had led to another, and she hadn't had time to have a quick reread of the Wranglers stories – she always meant to spend serious time on them and think of clever, relevant things to say. But somehow things happened. Like this morning and once again she had had to resort to listening to everyone else and then following up with a similar remark only slightly differently worded.

Sometimes she wished she hadn't joined the Wranglers, flattered by the invitation she hadn't been able to refuse even as her mind screamed What? A story every month?

A car hooted. Marigold put her foot down, exited the roundabout before realising she had gone round twice and was retracing her steps – then tried to think of a car alternative to retracing her steps. Retracing her route, she supposed, but now she would have to think about … oh bother … but she was near Dunelm and she had meant to go there … for … she was going to get … perhaps she would remember once inside! Turning neatly left she slipped into Dunelm car park and sighed as she engaged the hand brake.

Which was worse, thinking of a story line or deciding why she liked their stories? Writing a story wasn't too bad – she read a lot – and life was full of little incidents which made one think what next? So, writing a story was no real hardship although it was a little disappointing that somehow her story was always read first – or early on – and swiftly disposed of in a series of kind but superficial comments. But it was always all over so very quickly – and when you thought about how long it took to write and check – no, she should say edit – then you'd think they might talk about it a bit longer.

The worst bit was what could she say about the others' offerings? Always readable, sometimes she smiled at a turn of phrase – once she had actually laughed out loud! But at the end of the day, what could she say? Daphne sounded so very clever and sometimes, truth be told, Marigold wasn't quite sure – she would scribble a word or phrase down to Google later. Deborah's stories often seemed to have a hidden meaning, a depth, a hint of darkness – but how do you say that? After all, it might not be intentional. As for Priscilla, so light and frothy; life seemed all so very jolly, her plots would twist to reveal some hilarious solution … it was so very clever but quite how Priscilla did it was quite beyond Marigold.

Coming out of Dunelm, empty handed, she decided to go home and spend the afternoon Googling What makes a good story?

If only … she could find some intelligent comments.

Five Writers. Five women who enjoyed sharing their ideas once a month. Five women who loved their husbands, cared for their every need, but occasionally were irritated by some small quirk. And now five women who would have a niggling question … what can I think to write about before the thirtieth?

Only in the case of Priscilla there was an additional concern. And it would be no use whatsoever consulting the calendar on the kitchen wall beside the large pair of battered leather bellows. In theory, both Priscilla and Rupert noted any and all dates - dentist, car service, coffee with Pru, dinner with the Richardsons, pub lunch with Jim, sale at Exeter, fair in Northampton. Individual and joint – all dates would be noted. In theory. In practice it didn't always work out. Priscilla, despite her vagueness, was meticulous at noting each and any appointment or date. Rupert, on the other hand, claimed his casual commitments made for spur of the moment plans or cancellations, rearrangements or just plain 'forgot'. Buying and selling antiques and memorabilia meant he was constantly to and fro, in and out, or as Rupert admitted, 'flying with the wind'.

Sadly, when he wasn't 'flying' Rupert would be either plunged in deep gloom convinced business was about to crash or feeling exuberant with a latest success – if the former, he might spend time drinking despondently and become argumentative and the latter resulted in a desire for spontaneous often outrageously expensive purchases or equally celebratory spontaneous lovemaking wherever the mood might take him. And Priscilla. Not that she objected to the latter at all - but she had developed an allergy to fresh cut grass, had had a couple of nasty bruises from the attic stairs and was still overcome with embarrassment if she so much as saw the postman in the distance. Not to mention the trouble involved in cleaning tomato ketchup and whipped cream from the carpet.

If only … if only Rupert could be away buying some distant desirable item on the thirtieth.

Daphne watched Edgar wipe his lips carefully on his serviette. Serviette, she had to remind herself. Everyone said napkins, the shops sold napkins, Daphne had always said napkins but now she had to refer to them as serviettes. Edgar might be right that that was the original term – and one used in superior circles – but napkins was more friendly. More cosy. But trying to get that idea across to Edgar was water off a duck's back. He simply did not understand.

There was a lot she didn't understand about him even after all these years. He was kind and thoughtful, a good provider her mother would have said. If her mother were still alive, which fortunately she wasn't – her last few years had caused a certain amount of friction. It was obvious that Daphne as an only child should care for and support her mother as she grew more infirm but somehow it should not impinge upon their lives and routine. Her mother could not come to live with them, she deserved her independence, and the spare room was needed for visitors. Nor should she help her mother move into a Care Home; she had a perfectly good home in a desirable area – there was no sense in using it for care home fees while Daphne could travel over each day to check on her mother, make her a meal, keep an eye on the weekly cleaning lady … Avoiding care homes had been possible though a tad wearying on Daphne who loved her mother dearly, but wished Edgar could help shoulder the burden even if it were only loading the dishwasher. She had expected they would take a well-earned holiday once her mother had – mercifully – slipped quietly away but agreed that banking the money from the sale of the house made sense. For who knew what the future might hold?

If only I did … she thought more than once.

Wandering up and down the aisles in Tesco, Angela hoped in vain for inspiration. Consulting the list hadn't helped –

Tonight? Spag bol?

Thursday – 6 of us – slow cook – roast plus veg? – spicy chicken?

Bleach

Kitchen rolls and toilet

Garlic

Pudding/cheese ?

Spaghetti bolognaise was so quick and easy and at a pinch would do for tomorrow as well - could always bulk it out a bit. Trouble was David would probably raise his eyebrows and say Again? As if meals couldn't be repeated. And six on Thursday and no information at all was a tad risky with the spicy chicken – some people aren't the spicy type. But a roast – would need to be fairly large … they shrink … and would be more expensive so he would have something to say when he checked the accounts.

Not for the first time she wondered if a birthday voucher for a cookery course might not have been a good idea years ago; then he might be more understanding.

If only … she thought.

Browsing through Dunelm hadn't reminded Marigold what she had intended to buy, and it had made her homecoming later than planned. Which was a relief to Martin as he rinsed the wine glasses, gave them a perfunctory wipe before replacing them in the cupboard, it was a matter of seconds to drop the wine bottle among others in the recycling box and the coast was clear. In the kitchen.

Shortly afterwards Marigold found him seated at the desk, head in hands. In response to her 'Good morning?' He sighed, stretched slowly. 'Never stopped,' he murmured – which was true, oh so very true he told himself, smiling at the memory. Switching off the laptop, he stood, stretched again, bent to kiss the top of her head as he admitted to being 'starving' – it gave a chap an appetite, he smiled again, unseen by Marigold, head in fridge. She retrieved half a pie from the day before, put it on a tray with assorted fruit and cheeses, some crisps and a bottle of wine before heading for the garden. He followed with a couple of glasses.

It was relaxing, an al fresco lunch in the garden, both relaxed after a busy morning. Martin smiled gently as he asked how the writers' morning had fared. Marigold said it had been interesting … enjoyable. She never elaborated, being very aware that Martin, whose columns in a Sunday paper and regular contributions to assorted magazines gave them a steady comfortable lifestyle, regarded her writers group as something amusing, something to keep her occupied while he worked. At Real Writing.

Conversation lapsed as he turned the pages of the newspaper, she leant back, soaking up the warmth of the sunshine before deciding to get some sun cream and really enjoy an afternoon relaxing in the garden. Entering the bedroom, she looked at the tumbled bed, the lacy pants on the carpet and shrugged as she picked up the sun cream.

How long would this one last? He would profess eternal regret and love in the same breath eventually.

If only … she thought.

Andy checked the table. Stirred the sauce on the hob, then smiled as he heard Deborah's car crunch over the gravel. Lunch was light, just right on a warm day and he carried a tray of coffee out on to the patio once they had finished eating. Nothing much had been said – they didn't need to. She'd said everybody had talked a lot and he knew to let the silence relax her. Always aware and attentive to her moods and needs, Andy did it all without thinking now.

A blackbird inspected the edge of a flower bed, cocking his head when he paused. In the distance a tractor droned in some field. They sipped their coffee. The sun was warm on their heads as they sat on in companionable silence.

As the shadows lengthened Andy stirred, said he was thinking of making a start on that new bird table, the old one was just too far gone. Perhaps tomorrow morning. Deborah nodded, said she ought to weed the strawberry bed. Perhaps tomorrow. And they could drive over to the coast midday, have an ice cream and walk along the beach as a reward, he suggested. She laughed and said, 'Yes.'

Going indoors with the tray, Andy said he'd make a start making dinner early, his curry always tasted better after a long slow simmer. She nodded; said she'd check through the evening's programmes.

If only it could always be like this, she thought.

The Inspector tossed his briefcase on the desk.

'Ask Sergeant Wallace to come down,' he said to the constable carrying in three files.

'He left an hour ago, sir. Had a call. Body over at Tuxton. Sounded strange. Woman rang in – said he was dead and then kept saying If only'.

'If only?'

'Yes, sir. If only, again and again. If only … if only … if only …'

This piece is entirely a work of fiction. The names, characters and incidents portrayed in it are the work of the author's imagination. Any resemblance to actual persons, living or dead, is entirely coincidental.

ESTATE AGENT RAYMOND

He switched off his laptop. 'Another day, another dollar', flitted through his mind and out again; he found he was doing this occasionally and wondered if it were part of the grieving process. There were articles, particularly in the weekend papers, which he had read for a while after his grandmother's death and vaguely wondered if they applied to him. They were written to help - to ease the pain – to create greater understanding and acceptance – and while he could recognise some of the well-intentioned wisdom, much of it didn't apply to him. He hadn't fought against it, his grandmother had been old, in fact 95 could be considered very old and she had had a good life, difficult at times but as she would say 'Raymond my boy, at least I know I have lived '. So now he didn't regret her dying – he refused the euphemistic word 'passing' and would turn such pages without a thought. But he had noticed a propensity to think some of his grandmother's well-worn phrases – had even found himself uttering one or two aloud.

Picking up his notebook and mobile he nodded to Sylvia,

busy on her phone, and mouthing 'See you' left the office.

52 Park View was on the new development east of town and the morning traffic, such as it was, was mostly heading against him into town. Window open, the air was softer, milder. Spring really could be just around the corner he thought, perhaps he could get out into the garden on his day off and do some overdue tidying after the winter winds. In the meantime, Gary Smith and partner Mary Brown – he had a good memory for names and after listing the day's appointments usually did not have to refer to it again as he booked in two-hour slots when business was quiet. And today was a quiet day.

Gary Smith and partner Mary Brown were already waiting for him, car parked on the mini drive as if already taking possession. And he knew, even as they shook hands, how it would go. They had clearly read and noted every necessary detail from the glossy brochure and apart from a few questions – more to prove that they knew exactly what they were about – the viewing ran smoothly. Each room was commented on as they progressed, each cupboard and drawer opened, and the lift ladder lowered in order for Gary to assure himself that the loft was indeed boarded and fitted with a light as the brochure claimed. Raymond knew that they would buy it, knew how much they would offer, and he knew how much the seller was prepared to drop. It was like a formal quadrille, each dancer knowing his and his partners steps. He stepped outside to phone the seller while Gary and Mary toured their prospective home again. Stepped back in again to find them discussing how soon they could have their parents to dinner – perhaps a barbecue in their very own four metre square of back lawn - and advised them the price could be dropped by three thousand. As expected, Gary was prepared to up his offer by another thousand, thus they could all agree and sign on the dotted line … subject to survey, which Raymond knew would be a formality given the age and condition of the property and hands were shaken all round.

45 The Laurels was quite another matter. Cyril and Maggie Thomson, recently retired, looking to downsize and move nearer their son. Oh yes, the downsize. He quite understood the need to downsize but after viewing four previous properties although he had hopes for The Laurels, he knew the next two hours would be a constant list of regrets for what the Thomsons were prepared to leave behind and regrets that all they wanted to bring with them would not fit into a smaller house. Another bout of smiling as he agreed the benefits of downsizing, the perfect home the Thomsons were abandoning, the remote possibility that the move could create an enjoyable lifestyle – though of course not matching up to … Raymond knew how it would go and had already made a tentative list of three more possibles.

Cyril and Maggie were waiting for him too, car parked on the curved drive, in front of the substantial four-bedroom detached 1930's property. He pulled in behind them. The owner was at work, which was always a blessing, more so this time as he doubted Maggie Thomson would restrain her comments on decor and evident lifestyle; she hadn't so far. They toured the house and Maggie expressed her views on everything interspersed with the usual laments as to whether various items could be fitted in – Grandma's oak settle – so useful when – Uncle Toby's grandfather clock – such history … But gradually Raymond noticed Cyril was being more than soothing, he was being encouraging until his wife was almost agreeing that perhaps … just perhaps she would take another look upstairs while he went outside for a cigarette with Raymond. The sun was almost warm on their backs as they crossed the gravelled drive to inspect the garages. Taking a deep drag, Cyril exhaled slowly, 'Son showed me a short cut at the weekend – can get to the golf course in fifteen minutes from here – you should have shown us this first – still done no harm – maybe worn her down a bit' and he smiled for the first time.

Together they showed her the paved patio and expressed admiration for her suggestion that perhaps it was ideal for entertaining on summer evenings. The organised vegetable garden, already marked out for Spring planting, caused more than a passing interest when Raymond happened to mention that the owner had recommended her very reliable gardener. Encouraged to stand on the low wall near the pond, she was reminded of the view over the distant hills which could also be seen from the window of the master bedroom.

Raymond casually let fall the information that the owner was looking for a quick sale and there was a thoughtful look on Maggie's face when Cyril pointed out there was space for a conservatory … at that moment the sun shone with greater brightness and a robin burst into song on the apple tree.

It was not quite that simple of course but Raymond was pretty sure it was 'in the bag' when they insisted on touring the house again unaccompanied. He had time to confirm the text from Sylvia – lunch at the riverside pub sounded a good idea. And after a call to the owner, the Thomsons insisted on shaking hands when he agreed to meeting them back at the office immediately to finalise details. Sylvia was distinctly put out but agreed it was that kind of job.

It was worth missing lunch to have the Thomsons in agreement - neither party anticipated delays, the chain was almost non-existent, and Raymond set out with a light heart and a sandwich in his left hand for

The Shrubbery, which was out on the back road to a series of small villages on the west side of town. The back road was designated a B road but would have been a C if such things were allowed; however, the sun was shining, he had had a good morning and before him was an unknown. Owner Beatrice Forsyth had asked her nephew Eustace to organise a quote with a view to going into a Residential Home. Said nephew had intimated on the phone that his aunt was old, very old, not quite with it at times, a Home was increasingly advisable … Raymond understood, agreed a time. And here he was, the satnav confirmed he had reached his destination on his left.

Reached his destination - if it were in the middle of an overgrown patch of woodland. An entrance to a drive - or suggestion of – was just visible to the left of a large beech. Cautiously he manoeuvred his car past a large wooden crate, through the overhanging bushes and rounding a corner saw The Shrubbery. Parking next to a low-slung sports car and switching off the engine he stared in amazement at the house – must be early 1800's he thought – if it has any original features … At which point a young man came round the corner of the house, hand outstretched, 'Eustace Forsyth,' he said.

Explaining that his aunt might not understand some things, he ushered Raymond down the side of the house. 'Front door won't open, place needs a lot doing to it, probably too late,' and they went in through a side door, brushing the over-hanging ivy to one side. Beatrice Forsyth was sitting in an armchair by a window, propped up among several grubby looking cushions, a small table next to her had a tray and delicate china cup and saucer with still steaming tea. On the wide windowsill were several books and a pair of binoculars. She regarded Raymond with beady eyes and a bright smile, 'Eustace tells me you have come to give some advice about repairs. I think he worries far too much, I'm perfectly comfortable as I am. But do have a look round, and excuse me from accompanying you, I usually read the paper after lunch.' She indicated copies of The Times and The Financial Times.

And Raymond followed Eustace. The house was larger than it had appeared from the outside and he felt as though he had stepped back in time. Back in time – the furnishings – the décor (such as had survived) - and over all lay an air of neglect and decay. Eustace was at great pains to point out a damp patch above a window – 'Lord knows, what state the roof and attics are in', the peeling wallpaper in many rooms and the antiquated kitchen fittings. The dining room was clear out of 'Great Expectations' with the remains of a desiccated meal on the long mahogany table – 'She says she hasn't used it since her sister died …oh, about twenty years ago I think,' and the five bedrooms had wardrobes overflowing with clothes and belongings from family long gone. Old oil paintings in ornate frames hung on many walls and blackened silver jostled for space between large porcelain pieces. But behind the apparent neglect were the original cornices, mouldings, carved balustrades, leaded windowpanes - the list was endless.

Beatrice had prepared a tray of tea and seedcake for their return, explaining in response to Raymond's concern at her isolation that she left a shopping list and some money in the crate at the end of the drive every Friday and her next-door neighbour – 'at Willow Farm only four miles down the road' – picked it up and did it all for her. 'Daddy and his father were great friends,' she added.

The amiable conversation over tea took a nosedive when Raymond carefully mentioned in passing that while some repairs could be thought of as wise and an investment, if she were to consider moving to a more convenient location the house would probably, given its present condition, realise the sum of … whereupon Beatrice cut him short with a decisive, 'Never. My sister and I were born here and have lived nowhere else. I could not consider moving at all. I know Eustace worries about me, dear boy, but it's quite out of the question.'

Eustace putting down his cup, said he would stretch his legs, check on the oil tank and left the room with a frustrated expression. Beatrice smiled fondly, 'Dear boy. And he doesn't have to worry about repairs. I'm ninety-four, can't live for ever and I've had the National Trust visit. They are most agreeable to inheriting the house and contents − it will be part of their smaller period properties. I made my Will some time ago − Dr Martin was paying his usual check-up visit at the time - and they will carry out all necessary repairs and it is such a comfort to know that our home will go on for ever just as it is. My sister and I talked about it often, she would be so pleased. Please don't mention this to Eustace, he isn't very keen on preserving old family things − I hoped once that he would like some of the pictures and silver, but he says he lives in a modern world with modern things.'

Raymond restrained his smiles as he walked as far as they could in the overgrown garden where Eustace pointed out there was room for at least six to eight modern dwellings with garages and gardens, 'once I get rid of the old place'. Raymond nodded thoughtfully, thinking a NT tea garden could not fail in these peaceful surroundings and that he couldn't actually see any signs of loose tiles. He agreed he could suggest a tentative valuation in the meantime and that yes, he would be available for any future discussions as and when. Looking at Eustace' peevish expression, he crossed his fingers behind his back.

All this had taken some time, bidding farewell to Beatrice Forsyth they exchanged conspiratorial smiles, and he raced off down B123 hoping he would not be too late at

61 Acacia Avenue. But he was ten minutes late which had not suited Pete and Maria Wilson. At least it had not suited Pete Wilson, Maria therefore was more anxious than cross. She blinked nervously as Pete expressed his dissatisfaction at being kept waiting, brushing aside Raymond's apology, and added comment that he had preferred to keep driving than stop at a safe spot to phone ahead after the hold up on the bypass. Number 61 mid terrace was ideal for a couple with no children or pets and needing easy access to the town centre and the football ground. Pete approved the layout and general position; the parking space was more than adequate, 'and he knew a mate who owed him one and would lay a floor in the loft. Maria nodded in agreement as they viewed and once opened a kitchen cupboard – Pete told her it wasn't necessary as he had decided the kitchen met with their requirements. In conversation Raymond learnt that Maria didn't work – Pete said there was no need - and they had no family nearby – 'happiest on our own', said Pete - but she did like gardening – 'good job one of us has green fingers' said Pete, 'can leave it all to the missus.' Raymond said she might be interested one day in visiting the nearby church, which was well known for retaining its medieval herb garden, a left over from an earlier monastery. He did not add that they also had a flourishing Well Family Centre, as Pete said anything that might improve her cooking was welcome.

Acacia Avenue was fairly straightforward, it would be a short chain and would probably proceed to a satisfactory solution. Raymond was more than politely sincere in his good wishes: Sylvia volunteered at the local church Well Family Centre, and he had heard much about their support for wives in difficult situations. It had been, in more senses than one, a most satisfactory viewing and he proceeded across town to

Flat 44 Albion Place and being fifteen minutes early, texted Sylvia to suggest dinner at the riverside pub, smiling at her response. Mandy Spencer arrived with her parents, explaining that they were interested in her choice of flat.

Raymond had had several viewings like this one. Parents anxious about offspring leaving home, offspring desperate to be independent but seeking parental approval - and in this case, substantial backing. Mandy's father lost no time in making sure Raymond knew that he, in theory, was the prospective buyer. 'Nothing too much for my daughter' - except some privacy thought Raymond. The flat was spacious, well laid out, with a second bedroom – 'we shall come over most weekends to check that Mandy's coping on her own.'

Give her chance, thought Raymond. The balcony was small but had room for a small table and two chairs and had a pleasant view over the town and the river in the far distance. The owners were present for the viewing and conversation was somewhat stilted – as is often the case. They answered a few questions about the reliability of the two lifts and neighbourhood shopping – from father and mother respectively. Raymond was more concerned to discreetly position himself throughout the viewing. Thinking to himself, it was all very well to ask about lifts and nearby shops but how would you feel if you knew this is a couple about to split up and the wife has already two suspended sentences for attacking her husband with a kitchen knife (which was why he and husband ensured one or other was at all times between wife and her display of kitchen knives).

To his concealed delight it was yet another most satisfactory appointment, although he had some secret reservations about the safety of the husband after they left.

From Albion Place it was a short distance to the long Edwardian terrace not far from the town centre.

26 The Avenue was not on his official list; he had booked it with his friend's firm having been tipped off it was 'an interesting property just on the market'. The terrace looked as though it had seen better days, but a couple of houses had had replacement, but sympathetic, double glazing installed and three had clearly had permission to convert the small front gardens into parking areas and had had the pavements lowered.

The owner greeted him like a long-lost friend and was eager to explain he found it all too much since his wife had died, the previous year, he had found a suitable flat nearby and was keen to sell as soon as possible. He suggested Raymond look round while he fixed a drink, adding he hadn't been upstairs for some months – which perhaps explained the pillows and blankets on the sofa.

Raymond knew he loved the place as he slowly but carefully checked through the bedrooms and bathroom, trying not to note the hairbrush with long grey hairs among the feminine dressing table bits and pieces. The smeary windows let in enough of the late afternoon sunshine for him to appreciate the size and original features of the rooms. The bathroom made him shudder but realistically he knew it could be remedied with a complete refit. Descending the stairs, he was careful not to touch the banister rail and concentrated on the cornices and mouldings in the hallway below. Light through the stained-glass panel above the front door fell onto the tiled floor, highlighting sticky patches.

He could hear Mr Farrow moving about in the front room as he made his way down the long hall to the kitchen, glancing briefly into what had been the dining room judging by the furniture almost hidden beneath piles of papers and boxes. Overgrown elder bushes brushed against the glass doors and leaned companionably on the glass panes of the kitchen door. No chance of going out into the garden just then he thought, and turned his attention to the kitchen, which he expected to be small. It was hard to judge. These houses usually had small kitchens at the rear which could usually be extended.

But he could not concentrate, for once; his professional detachment deserted him. Every available flat surface was covered in stacks or small piles of used plates and dishes, half empty mugs and cups jostled with scatterings of cutlery and on the hob of an elderly electric cooker stood a pan of potatoes, their green sprouting leaves peering happily above the pan's rim.

Retreating to the front room he took momentary consolation in the original door finger plates semi obscured by a layer of white paint, before he was confronted by Mr Farrow proffering a half-filled cut glass tumbler of neat whisky in a shaky hand. As he confessed later that day, he could have downed it in one if it had not for the profusion of sticky finger marks around the glass.

Mr Farrow was a gentleman, accepted his apology for not drinking on duty and had it himself. Raymond, seated gingerly on the edge of a threadbare armchair, said he was more than interested and was sure they would come to an amicable solution. He could see beyond the present state and even before coming had calculated possible problems and costings. The price was reasonable, and he was not going to quibble, told Mr Farrow he would phone his estate agent with a view to making an offer and they beamed at each other.

At the little riverside pub that evening, Sylvia was a little disappointed that he had put in an offer, which had been accepted after Mr Farrow had consulted his solicitor, before she had seen the property too but said she understood the need for haste. They chinked glasses even as Raymond reminded her that his costings relied upon them doing much of the renovation themselves. Grandmother's legacy would be put to good use.

It sounds a worthwhile day for all concerned. But in some part will depend upon whether Gary Smith and Mary Brown discover that with the wind in the wrong direction, their garden activities could be constrained by the sickly smell of baking biscuits from the bakery on the light industrial estate nearby.

And as for the 45 The Laurels Cyril will be most concerned if he hears that the golf club is seriously considering an offer from a development company and the notion of relocating to a prime rural position.

You will, I'm sure, be delighted to know that Beatrice was judged to have been of sound mind when her nephew contested the Will and The Shrubbery is proving to be a successful addition to the National Trust, the contents alone being valued at over a quarter of a million. But then, Eustace had never liked old stuff.

Mandy did indeed move into her flat and her parents soon tired of the weekend commutes, leaving Mandy to travel back home whenever loneliness overtook her during the first year.

As for Raymond and Sylvia, they paid a fair price and occasionally invited old Mr Farrow to tea … after months of back breaking work.

FOLLOWED THE RIVER TO ITS SOURCE

Lionel and Emily were reliable fixtures in the village, had been ever since they moved in ten years earlier; appeared at every function or sent a suitably generous donation, entertained frequently and served on various committees and charitable bodies. Pillars of society one would say. And people did. Any need or problem and the murmur would go round - ask the Braithwaites. They meant Lionel of course.

Not that Emily didn't do her bit. She was on the WI committee of course, led the Church Ladies Flower Group, served regularly on the Protect Our Local Woodlands, was most active with St Johns Ambulance and the Guides and the Campaign to Protect Rural England, the local branches of the Wildlife Trust and the National Trust ... need I continue? The postman complained bitterly every December as he hauled an ever increasingly weighty bag into his van and was heard to mutter something about Christmas cards should be banned. But as old Grannie Smith remarked he should be thankful for his van, it was not like the old days before they even issued 'them there red bicycles'.

But why did everyone think of Lionel first? Because he was Lionel. Big and brash but thoroughly likeable. He talked a lot and knew a lot and shared it all in the cheeriest manner and with a generosity that was hard to match. In the summer he would offer one of his paddocks for the church fete and would patronise each and every stall. At Christmas a very generous donation to the Christmas Fete Fund ensured a very jolly event - and again, he would be seen to visit each and every stall.

Oh yes, Emily would be by his side - or near it - on these occasions. And she too would patronise the Homemade Fudge, the Hook a Duck, Knock a Coconut, Guess the Cake Weight and all the other fund raising ideas. But she was the quieter of the two. When he was there – as he very much was – she would smile and nod supportingly but was not often heard to actually comment.

They had no children and I once caught her watching the children's races with a rather wistful expression. She saw me look and immediately smiled brightly and clapped enthusiastically as Freddie Miles crossed the finishing tape with his egg and spoon intact.

So that's the Braithwaites – or rather was – popular and outgoing in our generally happy village. It was not perfect of course; no place or person can be. The downside was that the local bus service was only two hourly, and it could get rowdy down the pub on a Saturday night. Bill Twyns was known to do a bit of poaching on the side but, as it never got out of hand, nothing was said. Beryl Gates was known to visit Tom Brown later than is usual when her old man was on nights – but again, it was no one else's affair. Especially, as some said, her Bill stayed later than most after his shift.

So there you are, that's how we were in Little Middleton and doubtless that's how we'd be today if Lionel hadn't taken up with a new interest. It was always Lionel – except we'd use the Mr Braithwaite when occasions were a bit on the formal side. He'd had some new friends down to stay – heard all this gradual like – and talk had got on to clay pigeon shooting. Friend had suggested one of the paddocks would lend itself to clay pigeon shooting. Offered to introduce him to his local shoot, give it a try. And Lionel was hooked. Hook, line and sinker.

Must have cost a bit getting the licence and all the gear and so on, but as usual he was as generous as ever. Used to invite his new friends down once a month and made it clear to all the locals that he'd a few spare guns if anyone fancied a go. A few did. Occasionally. And a few had a grumble about the noise once a month, but it was only for one morning so it was generally agreed it could have been worse.

And I wouldn't have thought much about it except I happened to be serving the teas at the Christmas fete and the Braithwaites had sat down at a table in the corner with the vicar and his wife and what with taking over the tray of teas and then the tray of little cakes I couldn't but help over hearing Lionel talking about the new gun he had treated himself to – 'a double barrelled up and over Remington – a snip at £2,000' he said 'because it was second hand'. Saw the vicar wince a bit at that, but as the Braithwaites were always so supportive I suppose he thought 'Fair enough'. Emily just sipped her tea slowly, so slowly I thought to myself it would be cold before she got to the bottom.

Time moved on as it does. It was a bright crisp sort of winter, no snow but lots of frosty days - the kind that's supposed to kill off the germs and obviously one which suited the shooting fraternity. Lionel's clay pigeon shooting weekends began to be once a week and the shooting would last all day until the light began to fade. And his new friends stayed over for longer weekends. Old Jones was rubbing his hands as the weekly order grew (the Braithwaites had always supported the local stores – Jones used to get in things special for them). Must say that I noticed the noise often – sounds carry more on cold clear days – and you heard a few more grumbles down the pub. Though they stopped soon enough if Lionel brought his friends down and he stood drinks all round. Emily didn't come down with them I noticed. But then, his new friends didn't seem to bring their wives, if they had any.

Spring was coming in before it dawned on me that I hadn't seen Emily about much. Usually, she'd be popping into the church to help out with something, in the school to ask if they could use another something or other, or even in one of the shops. And when I did bump into her at the post office, must have been late March, she was coming out as I went up the path, so we only said 'Hello', but it did cross my mind that the winter hadn't suited her. Looked a bit drawn and peaky I thought.

Spring had blown in with cold wet windy days and we all huddled down to make the best of it. The clay pigeon shooting was cancelled more often than not but it was said that Lionel had joined a club, spent weekends with his friends and was becoming quite a marksman. Heard this when I was arranging the flowers one Saturday. Kate, Liz and I were early at the church and wondering how we would manage – it's not a good time for flowers of course and much has to be done with sprays of evergreens and ivy and they were talking about the latest news of Lionel and his hobby – when Emily arrived with a huge armful of lovely bright daffodils and narcissi. She apologised for being late – we'd dealt with removing the old arrangements and washing out the vases - said she'd driven all the way over to High Middleton to buy flowers from the florist there. It did cheer us up I can tell you and we were busy deciding who should do the altar rail and who should have the windows when I noticed the vicar walking out of the vestry with Lionel.

Vicar was nodding slowly while Lionel was rubbing his hands, smiling all over his face, ' ….. so, sorry I shan't be Reading at the service tomorrow but it's a bargain! It's a Purdey – one went for £100,000 last year – this one isn't quite in that league of course,' he laughed. 'But I've to drive over to pick it up tomorrow and it's a long drive. I'm thinking of competing more professionally now. Jack says now I've joined UKPSA I should consider trying for the …' and they were down the aisle and out of hearing.

I noticed Emily's hands were still for a moment on the tall vase, her fingers were thin, bony even I thought. And then she picked up two daffodils and carried on. Well, the church did look lovely even though I say it myself, and we adjourned to the vestry for a hot chocolate – except for Emily who said she had to be getting on. I thought again how thin her fingers were as she wrapped the red scarf round her neck.

Early next morning was dry for a change and the sun was quite warm on my back as I walked Max up the lane. And just as we passed by the Braithwaite's there was the sound of a gunshot; good job Max was deaf I thought, it startled me. I only take him to the end of the lane where it meets the B road; it's enough for him now. Vet says he's a bit overweight but he's getting on and we all put a bit of weight on then.

Except Emily, I suddenly thought. And perhaps it was because I was thinking about her then that I heard the sound as we passed their drive on the way back. It was the sound of – I don't know – not crying but a kind of wailing and banging. Stood and listened. It didn't stop. And I remembered that Lionel was going somewhere - had he left? - was Emily all right? It's a quiet village. We don't get break ins and things like that. And that's why it was strange to hear …

Thought I could walk up the drive a bit - listen out -

The noise didn't stop … the banging went on and on …

just a banging, banging … not right at all. And someone crying? calling?

Round the bend in the drive, I could see the garage door was half open and Lionel's car still there. Had he not gone? The noise continued from the garage - almost a rhythm to it. Going closer, Max pulled on his lead and I looked down and saw …

Well, an exaggeration to say a river but so startling in its red unexpectedness that yes, it was a river. I followed the river to its source. Lionel lay just inside the garage, blood still pumping from the mess that was - had been his head.

And the noise banging now in my head went on and on as I looked up to see Emily banging a gun - a Remington double bore up and over they said at the inquest - on the garage wall.

And the verdict was suicide of course. I mean it all came out then how much he'd borrowed and how the mortgage was more than overdue and so on and so on. So hard to believe, it had been going on for years.

And I sit here now, wonder sometimes if I'd done the right thing but when all's said and done what's the difference? Poor Emily, died within a few months. Cancer of course.

All she'd wanted was to go on a cruise in warm sunshine. But he'd wanted his Purdey and the chance to shine. Funny that. I'd have said he shone in the village, bright enough for us. Hadn't got time for a cruise he'd said. 'And something snapped,' she said. 'Wouldn't stop to talk about it. So, something snapped,' she said.

And the cruise would only have cost him time. She had her own money - not that any of us had known about that. Only came out when the school was told how they'd benefitted. So when all's said and done, best I'd kept quiet about how I'd found them and what she'd said.

Her memory lives on.

CLOUD BURST

He took his time digging the hole – there was no need for haste.

Pausing to watch a robin flitting to and fro in a bush nearby, he smiled to himself. That would be him soon … footloose and fancy free.

Taking the pickaxe, he set to again, loosening the large stones before heaving them up on to the edge of the hole. They were an unexpected bonus; they would prevent any fox nosing around from getting too close. The final neat bit – not that he had planned them – it was just fortuitous.

Oh, he had planned. Planned slowly and carefully with meticulous detail, taking his time, no stone unturned. The irony of that made him snigger briefly. After all, he had married the silly cow and endured her silly ways and was not going to waste all his efforts with one tiny mistake. Once he saw the opportunity, he knew it was all his for the taking.

Even then though, he did not make the mistake of rushing into decisions – much less any action. 'Slowly, slowly, catchee monkee' he told himself, quoting his grandfather who had served in India and had enthralled him with stories of far-off places and what sounded like exotic lifestyles leaving him with a desire to travel and sample rich living. Not a very probable step from the small three-bedroom semi, where he and his parents squashed in with his grandfather.

Time had passed as he moved out following one job after another, always slightly improving his prospects. But it was a slow process. Later his grandfather died and then his parents (rather younger than one would have expected but an addiction to cheap cigarettes and equally cheap alcohol in larger quantities than was advisable rendered it almost inevitable) leaving him a little money but no one who was really interested in him.

Life was … at best satisfying. Not what he craved … not what he deserved … but always, he reminded himself of his grandfather's advice – gained from experience when he and fellow soldiers tried to catch and tame local monkeys when life in the heat and dust of India palled.

And it paid off. By now he was in his early thirties, fairly good-looking, in a job which he could now term his 'career with prospects' and had learned to listen. Listen carefully … fill in the omissions … and reach a most satisfying answer. Cautious social contacts at work drew him into venturing to join the local tennis club – very limited members, but his boss was on the committee. And it was there that he met Drusilla.

She was everything he disliked of course – much younger, large blue eyes which had little expression, a silly giggle which grated and limited conversation. In fact, he had never had cause to exchange more than a polite passing Hello and that would have been that if it had not been for the cloud burst. It had put paid to any activity on court, of course, and he decided against lingering in the bar, waiting for the skies to clear. He would go home to work on the files he had waiting.

And outside on the steps he walked almost literally into Drusilla. A Drusilla so saturated her tennis shoes squelched, her long blonde hair hung in rats' tails – but the very wet shirt clung to alluring curves and he saw a new Drusilla. A Drusilla who for once didn't giggle but said quite simply, 'I walked up to meet the taxi – but it didn't come.'

And it was as simple as that. He drove her home – it was impressively large. Her mother already anxious, walked out to meet them as he stopped the car, insisted he come in … and, files forgotten, he had a very pleasant couple of hours. And went home, thinking hard. Reminding himself at intervals of his grandfather's catchphrase.

He kept it very low key … would offer her a lift home from the tennis club … almost as a casual afterthought (but having made sure he was there when she was there) and not asking her every time in case anyone remarked the fact. For a very brief while he actually toyed with the notion of paying attention to the mother – it was very brief. Mother in her turn, aware of Drusilla's limitations, made him very welcome, sought his advice on various matters and in a considerably short time they made a companionable threesome – he appreciated the mother's conversation, it leavened the very lightweight frivolous almost thoughtless level of Drusilla's contributions.

Tennis was abandoned – a combination of a cold Autumn and Drusilla's lack of progress despite the very excellent coach – and the three began to enjoy little cultural trips together. A day here and a day there became long weekends and Drusilla's mother was clearly congratulating herself on her daughter's future being in the hands of a caring and capable man, a little older than perhaps desirable, but then probably more reliable. And she herself enjoyed having the attention and advice of a sensible male, the only reasons she missed Drusilla's father.

Autumn progressed into winter and his plans developed, matured, were refined. By spring they were engaged and there was talk of a summer wedding – why delay? Why delay indeed? He had no nearest and dearest, and kept colleagues at arm's length and most conveniently – Drusilla and Mama had few relatives - and they were the Christmas card type. All three agreed they were perfectly suited and happy as they were.

A very small late summer wedding it was – and shortly afterwards he applied for and secured a better position – it did mean they would be living further away from Mama but their weekends together continued unabated. He was wise enough not to rub his hands in satisfaction … he could have been tempted to wring them but resisted and reminded himself of Grandfather's maxim. For living with Drusilla was far from easy, her vapid meanderings, when not diluted by her mother's down to earth conversation, were often very hard to bear.

Winter is not an easy season at the best of times, that one was a strain. A week away in a very plush hotel for Christmas was a great boost and he fixed his mind on the spring and the next stage of the game.

March may come in like a lion and go out like a lamb – but what mattered was May. And May cooperated by being almost textbook springlike. It was warm, flowers and foliage flourished, baby lambs frolicked in pleasant meadows, and they agreed upon a week in the Lake District.

Now the time had come, he was filled with regret that first evening as they sat at dinner. He had chosen well, the food was delicious, the rooms were comfortable, the nearby small town had just the right sort of antique and nick knack shops where the two ladies would like to browse … and he had purchased a small guidebook of suitable walks in the vicinity. He knew they could continue in this way indefinitely, but he had set himself a target.

The next few days passed very pleasantly – the only blemish was Mama showing an interest in the local baby shop and dropping a few gentle hints, from which thankfully Drusilla was easily distracted by talk of a new car (a panic reaction which could have cost him dear in the long run).

On the penultimate day they had a long and indulgent lunch – he explained he would catch up on the wine over dinner as he wanted to take them for a final drive up to a vantage point with spectacular views. And so it was that at four pm, when many tourists had gone to see the traditional local well dressing competition, the three of them had the spectacular view all to themselves. Standing on the high vantage point, he was at pains to point out famous landmarks. It was most unfortunate – a tragedy the local paper said – that Mama had leaned too far just as his hand, reaching behind Drusilla, had given that final push. Not a hard one – a hard one wasn't needed - and of course the post-mortem revealed that she had consumed a most unwise amount of alcohol.

Drusilla was not as heartbroken as he expected, in fact said she was delighted now that she had him all to herself and he found himself genuinely mourning Mama. But life went on – had to go on. Drusilla was diverted by the purchase of a new house – Mama's will had been predictable – and he found himself increasingly adept at setting her off on ever small new hobbies and interests. Most of which kept her safely at home when he was at work – they agreed they were perfectly content in each other's company and needed no one else. And he needed time to think, perfect the final details. For perfect they had to be. Not only had Mama's will been predictable, but it also revealed that there was a substantial inheritance for Drusilla which had been left in trust to her mother, about which Drusilla seemed to know very little and care even less. Having had a mother who had taken care of all detail, it was automatic that she should expect him to assume that role and happily signed everything placed in front of her.

He could hardly believe his good fortune and when Drusilla chattered on with little content and to less point, he would remind himself of the future to come. The future which would be more than he had dreamed of and which he must ensure was not at the slightest risk of failure.

He smiled again to himself, knee deep in the hole. It had taken time, and meticulous planning. Gazing round the garden - if it could be called that – he smiled again. The agent had commented briefly that the rear of the property was neglected but that should not be a problem as he was merely looking for a base from which to tour the area for a month and indulge his passion for photography. Neglected? It looked as though a bomb had hit it. The uneven ground sloped up from the back of the cottage with scattered shrubs and undergrowth to a steep cliff – part of the ground had been cleared and then left. Even now, water was trickling down the muddy slope after the heavy rain the previous night. Rain which had made his task rather messy. The ground was sodden, the soil thick and clagged but it had made moving the large stones easier, they were now piled unevenly at the side of the hole.

He paused to stretch his back, look up at the dark sky. He wouldn't be sorry to move on, leave it all behind him. It had been a tense few days, listening to her continual chatter while mentally checking and rechecking the details. And he bent to dig again, the hole must be deep, very deep so that any future work would be extremely unlikely to disturb what it held.

His farewell from the office, where he had not made close friends, had been simple and straightforward; he would be remembered, if at all, for a chap who got on with the job but was not very interesting. They had wished him well in Australia, joked about visiting for a holiday. The new bank account had been open for some time using the address of the flat he had rented some months ago, and where recently he had left all that he needed to start a new life.

As for local friends and acquaintances … it is remarkable how anonymously one can live in fairly affluent suburbia. He had been at pains to keep Drusilla focussed on their life together – her passing remark that she had wondered whether they should look for a local tennis club, reminding him how they had met at one and had such fun, had made him wince and caused him some mild anxiety. Time enough for that in the summer they had agreed.

So, his flat was waiting for him and his new life − he would move on from there very soon. Their house and contents were already with an estate agent for sale. This cottage and the rented car were in a false name − there would be nothing to link him with this place − not that anyone would be wondering. Drusilla had worried briefly about the car (safely garaged at the flat) needing a repair but had been more than mollified with the larger rented model.

He stretched again. All he had to do now was to bring her out into the garden.

Passing the bonfire from the afternoon before, he was pleased to see that everything from her shoes to her clothes to the silly books she read and all his belongings … all had burned down to fine ash which the rain had puddled in the shallow pit he had dug.

Carrying her body out of the back door, he paused to close the door behind him − the sky was overcast, and he had cleaned the cottage thoroughly, he didn't want to have to clean up a wet floor if it rained before he finished.

He was so close now. So very close to his new beginning, his rebirth when he could enjoy the life he deserved. Thoughts were swirling in his head, checking what he had done, had yet to do. It had been messier yesterday – not like the swift clean departure of her mother. But he had burnt the mat she fell on with everything else – a thin cotton mat, it had not taken too long. He had wrapped her body in the car rug, a small amount of blood had stained the part wrapped round her head.

Departing from his plan for the first time had slightly unnerved him. Instead of the wine and overdose of sleeping pills and final pillow smothering … he had snapped over dinner as she wittered on and on and on. That was the trouble, she could talk about any topic and never make any sense unless she were repeating some soppy paper she had read. Thinking back, he had no idea what she had been talking about, but the sound of her voice had dribbled on and on as he was nerving himself up for the final night.

When suddenly, he found himself seizing the heavy candlestick from the nearby mantelpiece and whacking her hard. Very hard. And again and again. Battering her skull and the long blonde hair into a tangled mess of blood and tissue.

Then stopped, as abruptly as he had started. Stared, appalled at what he had done. Time stood still and he was unaware how much time passed before he began the task of cleaning up. When he had thought, briefly, of how it would be, he had envisioned her seemingly sleeping form which he would gently fold into a rug from the car and then gently lay to rest. But he had pulled himself together. Made sure no blood was seeping from the rug-rolled body. Spent a long time washing down and cleaning every surface which could have had a splash of blood. Piled up and burnt the mat, her clothing, every item of hers, his bloodstained jeans and shirt …

Now it was time for the final act.

He carried her gently and laid her at the bottom of the hole, folding the car rug gently round her bare feet. Then began the slow and careful shovelling of soil down from the sides of the hole, pressing it carefully and gently round her. His clothes were filthy by now.

He had realised that he had a strong aversion to going back into the cottage, back to the scene where it had gone so horribly wrong. So, he had placed a change of clothing on the back seat and moved the car right down to the wood at the end of the long drive. No one came this way, so he had left the car among the trees, locked it carefully and returned to complete the job. Then he would rinse his hands under the garden tap, walk down the drive and into the wood, change among the fresh green leaves and set off into his new life with nothing to identify him until he reached the flat.

The body was covered now. He stretched and bent once more. The slight drizzle was rain now, heavier and soaking through his thin shirt, making the heavy soil more difficult to work in. His feet slipped occasionally in the mud now squishing up around his shoes.

He was not to know, the agent who gave him the keys and information did not know, that the previous year the owner had planned to develop some land to the rear of the cottage. Had hired a digger and made a start. But the land sloped up, old tree roots took far too long to grub out … and the project was abandoned … for later … perhaps.

Some of the old tree roots which had bound the soil together were no longer there to help prevent the disturbed and saturated soil from moving.

There was a crack of thunder, and a most unseasonable cloud burst when it seemed as if the very heavens opened and released a deluge of water – so sudden and so heavy that a large boulder was dislodged halfway up the cliff, it rolled down with increasing momentum and the disturbed land at the foot of the cliff slid, slowly, inexorably, and faster down the slope, across the edge of the garden. The torrent of liquid mud swept the heavy stones from the edge of the hole and knocked his legs from under him.

One stone cracked his head, knocking him insensible and then the whole was buried by more mud and uprooted bushes.

RETURNING TO THE FLAT

The cottage was pleasantly situated at the end of a lane, discreetly hidden by trees and bushes and generally neglected undergrowth.

It was one of the reasons Alex had been attracted to it in the first place – it promised seclusion and privacy. It had to be said – as the estate agent frequently did – that it had been sympathetically restored but the previous owners had not indulged in a whimsical olde worlde atmosphere. It was what it was; a solid comfortable large cottage with a substantial acreage which precluded any disturbance in the foreseeable future.

Ideal, Alex said, for escaping from the office and his small flat and a refuge after the regular long business trips he had to take. He did not elaborate, and the estate agent was left with the impression of a chap with a high-powered career and a discreet manner. A hint of military background perhaps in the close-cropped hair. Yes, the property would lend itself to entertaining – but he preferred to do that back in the city. Yes, it had room for a pony and would lend itself to family life - he thought his sister would visit occasionally but apart from that he had no plans.

And the village accepted that in its usual low key way. Newcomers could be a trial – remember that couple who set up Swinging Singles Sessions in the old farm under the guise of a health farm until the police were called to deal with a body? That new Alex Whathisname was known to have moved in, would be living there on and off, how much of which no one knew or much cared. All was quiet once the removal vans had departed. Alex Whathisname appeared to manage very well on his own - there had been no enquiries about a cleaner. He was seen from time to time stopping off at the local store, but Bill could only say he seemed a nice enough bloke. Didn't buy much – probably brought supplies down with him. Shame really, but there you are.

And time passed.

No major alterations were undertaken. No events occurred. Alex Whathisname was seen. And then not seen. The estate agent had let it be known that a very good security system had been installed but that was only to be expected in a remote place if it were to be often left empty. Some shook their heads at that extravagance,

Little Badley probably had a zero crime rate if anyone had thought to check.

There was a mild stir one weekend when a sleek red sports car swept in the direction of the cottage, a woman with long blonde hair blowing in the wind. Definitely a look of Whathisname – would be the sister. Sister left after two days and when Alex stopped off at Little Badley Stores on his way home the next day he was casually quizzed by Bill about his sister's visit. Alex had smiled wryly and commented that was big sisters for you – had to have a look even if he were not home. Yes, she had her own key. Yes, it was easier that way. No, they weren't very close but did see each other regularly.

And as sister was seen to come and go at intervals, it was assumed Alex Whathisname was home for her visits sometimes – or not. But it was nice they kept in touch, not like some families you read about.

And time passed.

Alex Whatshisname was clearly not inclined to get involved in village activities, but as they were few and far between no one took umbrage. The vicar, who flew between five parishes, was grateful for a donation and the annual agricultural show, held twenty miles away, didn't even know Alex existed. And if a couple of people had seen him driving up into the hills, it was assumed that he was either going somewhere or had a passing interest in the local area.

Life in the country tends to meander along, little disturbs the even tenor of the days. A storm damaged fence allowed a group of young and witless steers to gallop round the churchyard … the rising cost of tractor tyres … discussions whether the rising numbers of children might lead to the reopening of the village school … all attracted more attention round the bar in the Pig and Whistle than Betsy Hargreaves observation that she thought it a pity Alex Whathisname and his sister never seemed to go anywhere together. Bill's comment that Alex Whathisname's sister was called Felicity did make eyes turn. And a bit of a laugh at the fancy name. And how did Bill know? Oh, Alex'd stopped off to pick up a bottle of whisky, first malt too**,** had said, 'Felicity's down this weekend, better stock up'. The price of the whisky had been of far more interest. It was generally agreed he couldn't be short of a bob or two and the conversation was back to how many children were needed – it being agreed as always, that the little school had been the centre of village life and the bus journey to Big Badley ten miles away for five-year-olds was a shame.

And Alex? He was well pleased with his home and had settled into a comfortable routine.

Felicity too approved of the cottage. And she had a new man in her life … it must be admitted one in rather a long line. But that was Felicity. The new man was fair and slim – her preferred type. They had not known each other long – meeting online, time had passed as they exchanged snippets of information and by now matters had moved on to a meal together, and another meal. It was at the third meal – Felicity was in no hurry – that James suggested that perhaps she would like to have a meal at his flat the following weekend, he enjoyed cooking. She smiled sweetly, opening her pretty red lips in affirmation – and then paused.

Such a shame, she had promised to go down to her brother Alex's cottage to help with some research. Such a shame. And then, inspiration – 'Why don't you come down with me? I have to get started on Saturday, but Alex won't arrive until Monday. It's quite a pretty area and perhaps you could cook the meal you promised, and we'll have the evenings and nights …' and a flutter of the eyelashes.

It was all so easily arranged.

Felicity picked James up from his flat. And they were off. Speeding along the country lanes, once the hustle and bustle and queues of traffic were well behind, James felt himself relaxing and began to feel a rising anticipation for the coming weekend. Previous online dates had not been so attractive, so witty, had lacked the hint of spiciness to come. He might even be moving into something serious. Not something he had ever envisaged. The conversations over only three meals had been wide ranging and deeper than usual. This promised to be a weekend to end all weekends. He even found himself looking forward to meeting her brother Alex. And when Felicity turned for a moment, giving him that long slow smile before turning her attention back to the road, his breath caught in his throat for a moment.

Slowing down, Felicity turned into an overgrown lane which led to a low solid cottage, which gave the impression of quiet serene permanence. To the right of the cottage were two garages separated by a covered open area filled with wheelbarrow, lawnmower, boxes, garden tools, old garden chairs and more. The car stopped in front of the right-hand garage the door rising slowly as Felicity pointed the remote.

'It's a bit tight,' she said. 'If you like to get out, I'll just put the car away.'

James climbed out, stretching his legs after the cramp of the low seat and walked a few paces back. As the car eased into the garage, and the engine was switched off, he began to be aware of birdsong and the trickling sound of water before he stepped forward to help Felicity lift their bags from the boot.

The peace of the garden with its many white and pale-yellow flowering bushes, followed them into the cottage which smelt faintly of polish and … lavender? He followed Felicity through a large kitchen, ducking his head instinctively although the beams were high enough, through a wide room with comfortable deep armchairs and sofas and down a short corridor.

'Alex,' she indicated a closed door, 'Bathroom' and then, 'Us' as she opened the last door and he followed her into a room filled with deep orange, crimson and patterned fabrics. A large armchair filled with deep red cushions faced out into the garden. The contrast took his breath away as he dropped the two bags by the bed.

'Like it?' she whispered, slipping her arms round his waist from behind and resting her head against his shoulder. And then, quickly stepping away, she was back through the door calling,

'I'll pour us a drink and you can look round the kitchen. I'm going to bash out Alex's papers on his computer … you're going to make some sort of meal … there's bound to be stuff in his fridge, he's always prepared … and then we can … relax?'

The drinks were long and cold; James drank deeply as he inspected the fridge and cupboards. As Felicity had said, it was well stocked and he decided on a quick spicy Thai stir fry, but first he would put a toffee apple tart together and get that in the oven. Opening the kitchen windows to let in the fresh air, he moved about quietly and purposefully. The evening he was planning deserved a delicious meal first. They would need all their energies for what he was anticipating. He could hear Felicity busy in the sitting room where there was a desk and laptop under an arch and once, he stuck his head through the door to suggest another drink. Looking delighted, she joined him in the kitchen, admired the signs of his activities and this time, her embrace was longer and more lingering.

Only another half hour and she was back. Everything had slotted into place far more quickly than she had expected. Another drink while he finalised the meal? She was calling a halt on work for the day. There were better things to do.

The toffee apple tart was just crisping, and he began heating the oil in the wok as Felicity poured more wine. Raising his glass he called, 'To the speedy stir fry'. She smiled over the rim of her glass, inclining her head.

He had thought her odd to suggest a meal first, but as they ate, he felt himself relaxing more yet with a feeling of rising anticipation, the rest of the day would be theirs. The conversation was slow ... mirroring their relaxed mood, he knew he had excelled himself in the spicy flavours and by some fortuitous chance, the wine matched perfectly. He found himself telling her that he felt more deeply than he had thought possible, but she put her fingers lightly over his lips, whispered, 'Later,' and taking his hand pulled him to his feet. Surprised, he allowed her to lead him down the corridor to the bedroom, perhaps a bit too much wine, he felt a giggle rise but stopped it.

The curtains were closed, and the armchair was turned from the window, to face into the room. As he wavered slightly, she pushed him down into the chair, offered him his glass she had carried along and said,

'Relax - for the striptease.'

He lifted the glass, which was heavier than he

remembered, and turned his head slowly as she circled in front of him, dropping the scarf from her shoulders trailing it slowly over his knees. He swallowed, his tongue thick, took another sip.

She slipped off her sandals, flicking each one to the side with her toes. Slowly she circled, rising and falling on her slim brown feet. Unbuttoning her loose shirt, she let it slip down off one shoulder, then down on to the floor. Her hands cupped the lacy black bra for a moment as she smiled, running her tongue over her lips. He stared, breathing heavily. She circled again as she began to lower the skirt waistband down over her hips as she circled behind his chair. He lifted the wine glass slowly.

'Now for the pièce de résistance,' she whispered as her circling toes led her behind his chair.

It was the work of seconds to flick the garotte round his throat and brace herself, foot against the back of the chair as she held firm against his struggles. It was no competition; her wine had been watered and sipped. His – helped by a judicious amount of a well-known drug – ensured that his efforts were soon over.

She smiled slowly, humming lightly to herself. There were things to be attended to.

On Monday morning Alex stopped off at Little Badley Stores, commented he had forgotten milk and was there any of that delicious crusty bread he had bought a couple of weeks ago? Bill pointed out the bread rack, volunteering the information that it was made in the bakery at Big Badley and suggested that his sister would be pleased to see him. Alex shook his head regretfully as he left saying she'd texted to say she'd been called back for a meeting.

Bill shook his head at Amy Treadwith, browsing among the cards, and remarked he for one was glad to have a quiet life with none of this rushing to and fro. Amy Treadwith nodded in agreement and added that there didn't seem to be much in the Wedding Anniversary line.

Reaching the cottage, bathed in sunshine, Alex parked in front of the left-hand garage and carried the small bag of shopping in through the back door. Humming softly, he filled the kettle and switched it on. Put the milk in the fridge and the bread on the board, placing the breadknife and a crock of butter from the fridge beside it.

He walked through to his bedroom and ignoring the rolled-up carpet on the right, changed his clothes for a pair of old jeans and an even older sweatshirt and a pair of battered walking boots. And returned to the kitchen.

Taking a large mug of strong tea and a plate of thickly buttered crusty slices into the garden, he sat in one of the old chairs and leaned back, lifting his face to the sun. It was just what he needed after the long drive.

Later, only a few sheep raised their heads to watch him drive up the winding road into the hills; it was not a busy road, most people preferred the newer road connecting the market town Bubwith to the larger town Hargate which cut down travelling times. Alex had driven this way many times before, initially prompted by an old book he had picked up in a local antique centre in Hargate. The old book had woodcuts of limestone potholes and the mystery of their origins had not been well understood when the book was first published, but their mysterious charm and quaint names appealed to him. More research had revealed that while many such potholes and caverns had been explored and mapped there were some nearby which had not; they were believed to be comparatively small and of little interest.

Further exploration had followed, leading to the discovery of a couple (at least) of small potholes not far from the roadside. Alex had parked one day in a convenient spot and ambled about complete with rucksack, camera and binoculars.

One pothole was partially obscured by a few straggly low bushes; it was about twenty feet down from the roadside. He climbed back up to the car. Stood and admired the view, scanned it with his binoculars. The land rolled away from him, undulating to the east and west, behind him steep limestone crags and he could pick out the road below, appearing and disappearing in the uneven terrain. Not a soul in sight, only the wind at that moment blowing gently over the sparse grass. Curious, he walked back to the bushes and sat at the edge of the pothole, placing his rucksack beside him. Took the coiled cord, marked every ten feet with a red knot, from the rucksack and dropped the weighted end over the edge, carefully paying it out.

Now, Alex returned to that spot again and parked. Stood by the car and scanned the sky for birds, the hills for life, the road for movement. As so often before, all was peaceful and still in the afternoon hush.

It only took a few minutes to heave the rolled-up carpet from the back of the Range Rover, roll it down the grassy incline and over the rough edge of the pothole. And it was no more.

Returning to his flat a couple of days later, Alex inserted his door key, humming softly to himself. Let himself in, dropped his bag on the right and went into the kitchen to fill the kettle and switch it on.

It had been yet another perfect weekend.

WHO ARE YOU?

Conversely, who am I?

A question I occasionally ask myself when I sit alone drink in hand, book open unread on my lap.

The question 'Who are you?' will once again trigger a plethora of self-doubt in me, the daughter who never quite fitted in. I was never sure why in the early years; and in their defence, I suspect my parents were never quite sure about me.

And as if mirroring my doubt, the media on one hand encourages the delusion that there exists the 'normal happy family'; much of the advertising world is devoted to the happy family at work and at play. This despite the contradictory wealth of family drama and its attendant Soaps - which depicts and, at times, almost glorifies the families beset with physical and emotional disabilities or of murderous or criminal intent … the list is endless.

But how many, I ask myself, gazing into my glass, how

many have taken my route?

Early in life we – I had a brother and a sister – were very conscious of the fact that our parents regarded us as very special and expected great things (unspecified) of us. They gave us every opportunity and encouragement possible and yet success merited a cool acceptance. We would succeed where they had never ventured and yet I cannot recall any actual delight or excitement even in the early days when, for example, my sister won awards at ballet class and passed with Distinction each and every music exam, or my brother led his cricket team to victory and won rosette after rosette at gymkhanas. A 'Well done' or a 'That wasn't too bad' were the usual accolades.

It wasn't long before it occurred to me that my parents had regarded their family as complete with their pigeon pair, the perfect couple to achieve all their ambitions. And then I came along, later. Music and sport passing me by, I was soon aware that I didn't quite fit. It was most fortunate that I had academic ability and in the early days it came easily and naturally; after that I had the interest and determination to succeed. The latter was made even keener as I recognised it enabled my escape from the endless matches on the green sward; 'Well bowled, sir' a rare enlivenment. As for the concerts, while not too amateur, they were an equal boredom. Swotting for a Maths or other exam guaranteed my absence from many an event even as my siblings gazed at me with incomprehension writ large.

So far, so good. As Families went, I guess; although I rather suspected my sister would have liked a celebratory party upon occasion and my brother made reference more than once to a fellow competitor who had Firsts rewarded with a watch, a new bike etc. but we rubbed along well enough and accepted each other's foibles.

However, in retrospect, we were a happy family and seemingly 'normal'. My parents' encouragement and support continued and we in turn accepted their lack of emotional expression: it is only now I see its lack.

Childhood with its many happy memories. Teenagers with increasing abilities and widening social circles. Adults. That's where it began to slow and narrow and frustrate as realisation crept in.

No matter how talented, no matter how hard working and persevering, all of it counts for naught when the older years are reached. Dreams of being a prima donna, a concert pianist, making the England Eleven, the Olympic team … so very, very few achieve their dreams.

Setting their sights lower, Adam and Carla eventually had to accept the unpalatable fact they would have to enter the mundane world of work, their passions channelled towards less ambitious targets via 'a course? A qualification?' and a gloomy atmosphere pervaded the house.

I well remember Carla weeping after her first day in the bank, sobbing that her life was over. She always was the dramatic one. Adam bore his disappointment more stoically, but I suspected his tight-lipped reticence hid as deep a disappointment.

Not that they gave up, abandoned their dreams. Perhaps it might have been better if they had. Better than working in a conventional career, earning a low salary in a bit of a dead-end job but continuing to chase that elusive dream over weekends and every holiday. This was all over a period of time, of course. And me? I plodded on, seemingly without a dream of glory, starting work at a little-known research establishment.

Much time could be spent debating their choices, their progress – or lack of – but it would still be difficult to pinpoint the moment – if such it were – more likely a slowly growing awareness – when I began to see things as they really were. It began innocently enough, simply enough. Carla was convinced she could pull off an audition in Hollywood. Sam Whalley, the well-known director, was casting for a major film and the female lead had to be able to dance, to sing, to play the piano. She would lower her sights (?!) for a film role. Trouble was, the bank did not pay well enough and she would be taking unpaid leave. I stumped up of course, being more than willing to help.

It began then. I think. Or perhaps not. Does it matter?

One by one, over time, their requests, their pleas, demands dripped down my phone, popped up in my Inbox and as I was by this time, well able to assist, at first I didn't mind. Initially, it was Carla and Adam trying for first this break and then that and I admired their persistence for a long time. Felt their disappointment, shared their hurt, wished them well. Then Mum wondered if I could help out with a new automatic car, 'A bit too big an investment at our age,' she said, 'but it's a necessity now that Dad's crippled with arthritis and I'm not too spry.' Again, I was more than willing. Dad thought that Mum deserved a break, he felt guilty about how much care he needed. 'A couple of weeks in the sun,' he suggested. 'Might be just the thing to perk her up.'

The requests ceased being requests at some point.

It began to be assumed that I would be there to foot whatever. We drifted on. I didn't actually see that much of them by then; my work at the research centre kept me pretty busy and then the trips to conferences never seemed to slow down, if anything they increased.

And so it may have continued, how long for?

If William had not been posted to Tokyo. Permanently.

We had always worked well together and over time shared ideas and confidences over a meal or on a long flight to some meeting. So I knew I would miss him. A lot. And was not surprised when he suggested a meal the night before he left the office for good. He said he had booked a table at Gigliano's and would meet me there at eight. Carlo gave us our usual table. The meal as usual was perfect. And the thought crossed my mind that this need not be for the last time. William would be back for some meeting or other. I had had the offer of a couple of research contracts in Tokyo but had never felt tempted enough. Yes, it need not be our last meal together. I could always pop over to visit. I sighed, meanwhile I would miss William.

He had been quiet for a while, slicing his dessert into ever smaller pieces but not actually eating. Put his fork down, took a slow drink of wine and said –

Said –

Said he had enjoyed working together, had always admired me – and my work he added hurriedly.

Said time was moving on and now he was in his thirties, knew it was time to settle down.

Said that for that reason he had asked Felicity to marry him, she loved Japan, had worked there.

Said he would miss me and wondered once … and was quick to add that I had my close family connections, he had always admired my commitment.

I don't remember what else he said.

The rest of the evening was a bit of a blur to be honest. As I recognised how much I would really miss him, how there had always been a faint dream that perhaps one day …

Well, William went. And I had other colleagues who

were cheerful, encouraging – who were friends too. But I knew I had lost something important, someone special, someone I had relied on more than I had realised. Slowly, a small resentment grew. If I hadn't spent so much time thinking about, helping, whatever, my family, perhaps I would have been able to focus on what really mattered for me.

For family were still there of course. The calls, the emails, the ideas, pleas, demands, maintained their steady drip. It wasn't the money. Really it wasn't the money. Well, not really. Somehow, I had taken a mental step back and looked at how we were , where I stood in relation to them. Adam and Carla were never going to achieve anything major. In fact, Carla sometimes looked - just a little bit – perhaps ridiculous or desperate – reaching for parts she was too old for. I'm not being unkind, just realistic. My parents were aging of course and relied on me for every bit of help and advice; and I thought back and wondered how encouraging had they been, how much interest had they shown in my achievements? It seemed as though they had just taken me for granted – first as a child who did not fit into their dreams and then, now, the cash cow.

A phrase I had not known I knew. Until it surfaced in my mind.

They say blood is thicker than water. They say family ties are the strongest of all. Perhaps in some instances. Sitting here now, I can tell you that it just is not always so. As the weeks passed my resentments grew and yet I could not walk away, sever ties completely.

Summer was hectic, pressures at work. Carla desperately chasing the occasional break which came her way and in-between bemoaning her lot, increasingly convinced fate (or a particular agent) was conspiring against her. Adam had invested heavily in a racehorse – now that he had so few opportunities to ride for a patron – it broke a leg but instead of feeling pity for the animal, immediately got involved in another cert. My parents decided they should have the garden landscaped to make it easier to manage.

By September we were all frazzled. And I knew it had to end.

My suggestion that we share a holiday cottage by the sea for a fortnight was quickly accepted – I was paying of course. This was the moment I thought, we would spend time together, relax, talk things through, they would see that we would have to make some changes.

I made the booking through an agent, too busy to even wonder if it might live up to expectations, photos can lie. Adam was driving Carla down; I would pick up the parents on condition Adam would drive them all back. His car was certainly big enough! I listened to my mother's gloomy prophecies all the way down – not that she seem concerned about my possibly wasting my money, more that her bed might not be comfortable, that the view might not be as promised, there might be noisy neighbours, she preferred Sainsburys to Tesco but had found no trace of either locally … All the way down I listened, making consoling noises after my father fell asleep. More in protest than anything I suppose.

Contrary to her doleful prognostications, the cottage was delightful. Just as promised. The brochure had not lied one jot. Mother was impressed by the size – she had been convinced the cottage would be tiny. The bed was declared quite satisfactory, and the absence of any near neighbours was a bonus. Father cheered up visibly at every declaration. Adam and Carla helped me to unload both cars – we had agreed to take enough provisions for two days until we had time to survey local facilities. Though Carla pointed out (often) that the point of a holiday was eating out rather than doing any home cooking.

As we had stopped at a pub on the way down, it was agreed a barbecue would be very nice on our first evening. Adam volunteered; Carla offered to clear away. And they both agreed that they were looking forward to sampling local hostelries – perhaps I'd like to Google a few?

While they pottered about, drifting to and fro with bits and pieces to the brick barbecue at the end of the garden, parents were comfortably ensconced in front of the TV with a pot of tea and plate of biscuits. I settled down to read the Cottage Information file.

The agents had not exaggerated. So far, it had lived up to its promises of space, facilities, comfort, conveniences etc and there were leaflets for near enough attractions – mainly National Trust.

I leaned back and thought. We would relax and gradually I would bring the conversation round to how we saw the future. What did we hope for, what would we like, what would be realistic? Perhaps in the evenings, all together as a family, as we hadn't done properly, for a long time.

Ha! Well, that was then. Over a week ago and I had tried, my God how I'd tried. There was just no getting through to them. Each and everyone of them was deep into What I Want, not even what I Would Like. As for me, I was all right, wasn't I? I had my wonderful job and prospects (not even a well done Fenella) so there was no need to consider me. When I mooted the scenario of supposing I wasn't around - a tragic car crash? They waved that aside as totally irrelevant.

I think Adam began to have a faint inkling of how I felt but quickly adopted the tack of I should be grateful for the start in life that our parents had given us, it was my duty to respond in kind. Yes, I could have pointed out that he and Carla were not my parents so where exactly did they stand in the equation?

But a great weariness overtook me. I let the conversation waver, falter, picked up on the planned excursion for the morrow, said I would prepare the evening meal. After days of dining out, we had agreed on an MnS selection, all to be conveniently heated up together. It didn't take long to prepare and as it was chilly, we sat together round the large table in the kitchen. Adam opened the wine he had chosen and I laid out the desserts, cheese and fruit on the side.

MnS are so reliable and good value for a quick easy meal at home. Even Carla could not complain aloud about having to cook (I did sometimes wonder what exactly she ate at home). The September evenings were drawing in slowly, so I moved the small lamp from my bedroom to the corner worktop in the kitchen. It was as if the earlier conversation had been completely forgotten and as I gazed round the table in the low lamp light, I felt a warmth momentarily. They ate slowly, savouring the food and wine, Adam topping up before the glasses were drained. Carla was mimicking a well-known TV personality and as the shadows lengthened, I sat as if watching a play for my benefit – see what a lovely family we are altogether.

I removed the large plates, rinsing them with the cutlery before placing them in the large bowl to the left of the sink. The puddings, cheese and fruit were piled in the middle of the table and there was a slow contented sampling of each; by now Adam was describing some murky episode at a well-known stable, and everyone hanging on as each salacious detail was related. Suddenly, Mum shivered, 'It's chilly,' she said. 'Get me a cardigan, will you?' looking at me.

As I walked down the corridor, I heard Adam say he'd put the heating on for a while, it was a bit nippy, and I heard the boiler leap into life in the corner of the kitchen. Located Mum's cardigan, which was never far away even in the height of summer and took it back. Laid it over her thin shoulders, she smiled a Thank you, eyes on Adam and the finale of the stable saga. He opened another bottle as they all roared with laughter and Mum

245

added her usual 'Well I never, who'd have thought it?'

It was one of those evenings when enjoying food and wine and a good story, everyone was relaxed and happy and contented. I wondered if they had any idea how alone I felt. They were happy with their lives, and at that moment had not a thought for the morrow. But there was no need, Fenella would make sure it was OK.

Fenella was there but not there. She was listening and watching but not part of it. I just did not belong. I hadn't said a word for ages, but no one had noticed. Wondered after a while if they had all had a bit too much to drink, conversation was slower, and the lively chatter had died down to a long rambling account from Dad about the day he first met Mum. We'd heard it all so often, always over Christmas dinner. She was nodding slowly, smiling to herself.

I said I was going to get my phone, thought I'd take a few photos, opening the door into the corridor, glanced back, you'd think the perfect family group if you didn't know the whole story. Closed the door to keep the kitchen warm and headed down to my bedroom. It had been a good idea to ban phones from meals, I thought, Carla had managed, and we had all been spared her histrionics if her agent called. The curtains fluttered, it was actually cold now and I went to close the window slightly, couldn't bear to sleep with it completely closed. Rummaged in my bag for a Paracetamol, as I checked my phone … a slight headache niggled behind my eyes. Checked my phone, a few emails, read them through but they could all wait to the next day for a reply. After all, I was on holiday. Decided to go to the loo after taking the Paracetamol with a swig of cold water, was in no hurry to re-join them

All was quiet in the kitchen; they were all still sitting at the table. Mum's head had drooped until her chin rested in the folds of the cardigan sleeves I'd crossed in front of her. Dad was leaning sideways on to the corner cupboard, a thin dribble glistened on his chin. Adam and Carla were sprawled heads on arms on table; Adam's head rested on the remains of his roulade while Carla's head was on one arm which was curled round a fallen bottle, the last drips soaking into the checked tablecloth.

They say time stands still.

It does.

But not for long.

In the corner, the boiler murmured gently on. The room was faintly stuffy. I looked round the table again. And closed the door.

But I didn't switch the boiler off. Not before and not after I'd closed the door on them and walked away. And went for a walk in the garden. The night was still and dark, lit by stars above and glows from the cottage windows. The chilly air was refreshing as I breathed deeply. The headache still niggled but was easier. Perhaps the kitchen had been too stuffy and I'd drunk too much. I thought that. But didn't believe it.

Who are you?

I gave my name and address. Said I needed help. The voice said they would be with me shortly.

And so, I repeat Who are you? and ask myself Who am I? that I could walk down the lane listening to the murmur of the waves and back again. That I could open the porch door and take a coat from the nearby peg and walk down the lane again. And back again. That I could sit in the summerhouse, arms wrapped round myself, thinking nothing. Only that I would wait for daylight.

There have been no sounds, no movement.

Only now the faint sound of a siren wailing in the morning light. I shall say I went to bed early.

THE DIARY

Great Aunt Augusta - always referred to as GA Augusta in our rather voluminous family correspondence - was actually a rather pleasant person despite the rather forbidding title. Although seemingly devoid of humour she had been known to add to the gaiety of one nephew's 21st by dancing on a table singing a raucous well-known ditty accompanying herself with two large silver serving spoons (much to the distress of aforesaid nephew's maternal parent). Sadly, the occasion being captured on film – this was long ago - and having inadvertently seen the photographic evidence, she could never be tempted to partake of more than one sedate glass of wine at any subsequent family gathering.

Perhaps it was just as well. GA Augusta married an ambitious diplomat and any dancing on tables, much less doubtful carolling would not have been an asset. I gathered from family conversations her parents had despaired of her marrying well and settling down; her teenage years had been somewhat unconventional while she tried in vain, but with great enthusiasm to become a

National Hunt jockey. Fortunately romance intervened shortly after the Spoons episode, as it was frequently termed, and all boded well. And so I only knew her as a pretty but rather dignified person who only seemed to unbend over family meals.

Her husband was somewhat older but charming – as diplomats tend to be – and GA Augusta's enthusiasm turned abruptly from horses and to 'being an asset'. They travelled widely and were posted to remote and fascinating places which appeared in the Press from time to time and where most unusual incidents seemed to happen. There was the case of the coffin, stuffed with bank notes, fortuitously opened by mistake at the crematorium just in time to avert the fall of the Government in a small but important South American state. Although the body, of the unfortunate member of the Opposition party ,was never traced.

As the years passed, William and GA Augusta moved on into more exalted and rarefied circles from Paris to New York, from Zurich to Moscow with – to my great delight – long leaves spent with my parents, deep in the Cotswolds. They said the peace and tranquillity of the countryside gave them rest and strength for the next posting. As a teenager somewhat disenchanted with country living, I found this hard to believe. I would listen in awe to conversations round the dinner table as well-known names were bandied to and fro – not only politicians you understand, but celebrities of various kinds also frequently appeared to grace some social or diplomatic occasions.

It gave me a secret sort of thrill to learn that B… C….. was unpopular on film sets because of his habit of continually spitting, that the President of M…… had an ingrowing toenail which was why he refused to inspect the guard of honour almost severing relations between the two countries, the wife of the Prime Minister of W….. was caught in flagrante delicto with the butler in the F….. Embassy … These stories were always accompanied by 'Of course, this is in strictest confidence …' so force of habit compels me even now to use initials. William was a dry but amusing raconteur, frequently turning to GA Augusta, to corroborate some detail.

GA Augusta enjoyed rising late – William preferred to accompany my father round the farm before breakfast – and I would be deputed to take up her breakfast tray. I quite enjoyed this. She would ask me to sit on her bed while she commented on the day's headlines usually with a juicy titbit thrown in. I began to add an extra cup to the tray, and we would have a most enjoyable hour together. Her life was all that I could dream about – travel, famous people, important events – they had no children, and I began to hope I would be invited to visit. A flight to some far-flung outpost would do. A flight to a major world capital – words failed me. I would fall asleep at night dreaming of the Maybe One Day.

During breakfast one day GA Augusta asked me to open the top drawer of her bedside table and pass her her Diary. It was a fat book bound in crimson leather with small brass corner plates and screamed of Exotic Places and a Life Lived doing Wonderful things. I said it was an attractive book. 'Marrakesh,' she replied absently as she turned a page. Marrakesh! My heart beat faster. Would I get there one day?

Their visit ended shortly after that and they disappeared off to Tokyo for what proved to be a protracted tour, University rescued me from the local Young Farmers and Life became hectic as it does, it was thoroughly enjoyable with ecstatic and heart-breaking moments at bearable intervals. Miraculously I'd picked the right course and life became even more wonderful as a career opened up. Home became more of a stopping off place, so I only saw GA Augusta and William briefly at intervals, although I heard from various family sources, that each interesting assignment produced more wonderful stories.

Life has a strange ability to somehow change both speed and time. One minute I was sitting on GA Augusta's bed listening to what the chauffeur had really done with the turkey as I passed her Diary and the next minute my father was gently breaking the news that there had been a car crash. Had it really been ten years?

You get through the days of course and the words grief stricken and devastated seemed rather over the top, but I was only one of the many family members and friends who packed our local church. Sitting beside my parents I regretted that somehow there had never been time to see more of GA Augusta and William, making a silent vow to visit my parents a bit more often.

A few weeks later a package arrived with a note from my parents. GA Augusta had left me her string of pearls, an emerald ring, a thousand pounds and her Diary '… I remember Polly admiring it long ago.'

Her Diary! Stuffing the small jewellery boxes back in the package I hurried to pour a glass of wine and settled down to start reading of GA Augusta's adventures round the world.

And there my story ends.

Page after page listed details of the weather, the rising cost of petrol, the length of a flight to somewhere compared to five years previously. It was not a whinge. She did not bewail being marooned in a typhoon off Honduras on a small island; it was noted as a fact. Was she so accustomed to typhoons that the ferocity of the wind merited no mention? Did nothing blow over or away? How many roofs flew by?

Weeks, months, years passed with incidental detail noted as worthy of mention. People and events were noted as dates but of shared confidences or what she really experienced and thought of it all …? Not a word! The stories round the table had promised so much more but they were all I had.

Oh, and now? I found the actual book was removable so I'm now the proud possessor of a diary in a rather battered leather cover with brass hinges. And it makes better reading although I haven't travelled far or met one celebrity yet.

MARRIAGE IS COMPLICATED

A lot later than usual, Agatha opened the kitchen door, stepped outside, and shook the tablecloth over the paved yard then stood still to enjoy the flurry of sparrows tumbling down to the scattered crumbs.

One of her favourite moments of the day, especially when the yard was warmed by the early sun. I say one of, Agatha had many favourite moments every day. If asked, she would probably have said that was how she had been, as long as she could remember. Enjoying waking up to see daylight edging the bedroom curtains … soaking her face flannel in hot water and then holding it to her face for a few moments … the first sips of morning tea while she waited for the toast to crisp … the sparrows chittering among themselves as they waited on the low wall near the kitchen door …

And so it went on − so many little moments in the day when she felt pleasure. Only now, Agatha was able to savour those moments for a tadge longer if she so wished, several moments indeed occasionally. When Albert was alive and the farm was still a working farm, there had been endless happy moments but usually fleetingly noted in the midst of a busy day. For life was always busy on a one-man farm, they could only afford extra help at lambing and hay time; although as Albert often said, there was no need otherwise, he was perfectly capable of managing on his own. (They did not consider mentioning the sheep shearing team, who were a Spring fixture on all the local sheep farms dotted around the moors).

Plus, he had his Agatha – his 'helpmeet' as he would term it when he sat savouring the Sunday roast. 'Where would I be without thee? My one and only helpmeet?' And he would raise his glass. Agatha would shake her head and say, 'Get away with you, man.' But she liked it; you could tell. And she would proffer one of the vegetable dishes again.

The Sunday roast was a firmly entrenched tradition. Even during the war when times were hard, Agatha managed a tiny roast which lived on as 'cold on Monday' washday, meat and tattie pie on Tuesday … which on occasion lasted into Wednesday but there would be nothing left of it for Thursday. You might be thinking 'Why not indeed – they had sheep', but it was not as easy as all that with the Ministry of Food's inspectors checking on flock numbers etc. Of course, a sheep could break its leg out on the fell … a chicken might drown in the water trough – they were foolish creatures … rabbits were fair game … as were pheasants … so, as I said, the Sunday roast lived on. Even when one of God's creatures did not.

They were hard but contented, happy years. And Agatha had her extra happy moments; much as she savoured them, they were a very private affair and she never thought to share them nor enquire whether Albert was equally blessed. For she very much regarded it as a blessing – to recognise a moment which gave her pleasure, sometimes so intense she felt she was hugging it close, noting it for a memory to be recollected at some future date.

Those years were long gone now, like Albert, her helpmeet. He had died peacefully in the garden one Sunday afternoon. He had taken his unfinished glass of beer out into the sunshine, saying he would sit a while before checking on the old ewe in the orchard. Agatha had said she would stack the dishes and tidy round then sit a while with him, only she would have a cup of tea.

It had comforted her a little, to know that he had known she was coming to join him. 'But not like that' she had involuntarily exclaimed when she stepped out to see him sitting back, in his chair, head lolling to one side and Jim, sitting close, head resting on Albert's knee and eyes gazing up at the peaceful face. When she sat in the adjoining chair, still clutching the mug of tea, Jim moved to rest his head on her knee, and she stroked his head as she thought what to do next.

What to do next moved on in the blur of steady organisation as so often happens when you have thoughtful family and good friends.

And it had worked very well for a few years – except when Agatha missed her helpmeet and had a little weep, but as she never mentioned this to anyone, life moved on. For as she said to herself, that's how it is … now … and I do have so much to remember … and be thankful for. Jim too had stayed on, her companion for some years. Sons and daughter visited when they could but did phone regularly.

Until we reach this morning - when Agatha had shaken her tablecloth as usual for the sparrows – several generations down from the first, who had spotted her early morning routine. She had had breakfast much later than usual; a change of routine which had been creeping up on her for some time. Both sons and daughter had made alternative life choices and worked far away, they were more than happy to see the land sold off in parcels to neighbours and Agatha able to stay on in the farmhouse with enough to live on fairly comfortably.

So, moving on, they were all 'in the loop' as she had learned to say and also in agreement – that in the not-too-distant future it would make sense for Agatha to move into a small convenient house near the edge of town. Hence the late breakfast. She had slept rather badly, thinking what she would take … what she would like to take but would be impractical … and what should 'go'. She had wandered round the house – mentally – and visualised each room saying to herself 'Yes, take that … no, no use at all in a small house … never really liked his mother's chest …' and so on until she fell into a restless sleep.

And sat over breakfast longer than usual until the chatter of impatient sparrows moved her to the door. Back inside again, she folded the tablecloth, placed it in the top drawer of the Dresser. And stroked it affectionately. She loved the soft shine of gleaming wood. The patina of years she thought. A bit like me, only I don't shine. The Dresser had been in the farmhouse when Albert first took her to meet his parents. His mother had made a point of explaining that it had been there when she had first arrived as a young bride and Goodness knows how long it had been in the family. Agatha had nodded politely, smiling as she inwardly shuddered at the sheer

261

size of the thing. Looming up to the low beams, the Dresser dominated the kitchen, large though that was. And all the time they lived in the cottage down the lane, Agatha secretly plotted that when they inherited, the Dresser would be the first thing to go.

But times and people change. By the time the old people had gone, and Albert and Agatha moved in – with three rumbustious children – she was the first to admit that its capacious cupboard above and drawers below were the most practical and useful storage. Instead of her mother in law's kitchenalia, Agatha making use of its location by the back door, had allowed it to fill to almost overflowing with jackets and socks, mitts and gilets, scarves and sweaters etc. And its sturdy construction and very age meant she hardly noticed when Tommy crashed his tricycle into a corner or Belinda slammed its drawers shut in frustrated teenage years when a favourite hat or mitts or bag could not be immediately located.

Dresser lived on, its quiet dependable character increasingly appreciated – until this morning when Agatha realised with a rueful dismay, it would not suit, much less fit into a small townhouse. And she would miss it. Nor could she pass it on, all three children had said it was a Family Heirloom … but, no thanks. Would not belong in their ordered sleek modern lives.

Agatha absently patted its left door as she slid the top drawer open, took out pad and pencil and looked round the kitchen to start her Moving List.

Wrote MOVING LIST in capitals. Underlined it.

Put pad on table, switched on kettle. Best to start with a coffee, helps one think. Waiting for the water to boil, she opened a few cupboards, peered in the larder and by the time her coffee was steaming on the kitchen table she had listed -

Half the blue china (she was *not* going to host large family gatherings anymore)

Windsor armchair (it would *have* to fit)

Some table linen (again not all)

The morning proceeded slowly from room to room, cupboard to cupboard, drawer to drawer and the list grew slowly too as she began to realise how much she could live without. There was little hope that the family detritus which had drifted into pools and piles around the house would be claimed – they had taken what they wanted long ago. The solution would be a House Clearance firm; Agatha had watched her TV and read her magazines enough to know such firms existed.

Tommy, when consulted, said what a sensible idea and rang back to say he had located a nearby firm online. And hurriedly explained he had found the firm online but she, Agatha, would not have to do anything online – would she like him to phone and arrange a date? Oh yes, she would and before the end of the day, he had rung back to advise her that Shottely and Sons would be over to give her a quote Friday week. Agatha carefully noted both name and date on her fridge memoranda. And made another cup of coffee. Looking at the Dresser she said, 'Suppose you'll have to stay – part of the fittings and fixtures.'

The following week was a heady mix of nostalgia – for many happy times – and a certain growing excitement as Agatha contemplated the prospect of a move and a new life. The thought of the latter created a brief fling with a foreboding of uncertainties … doubts … apprehensions at the unknown … before she gave herself a mental shake and good talking to as she made a cup of tea at 3am one morning. Agatha was a practical person. After that brief hiccup she busied herself with tidying cupboards, sorting through drawers and boxes, making a bonfire of paper and boxes 'which might come in useful' but as they hadn't could be disposed of quite early. And Lists. Ah, the Lists. Added to, crossed out, made again.

'Taking' - was longer than she liked – not because she didn't want items, it was more that it meant less room for

'Possibles' - which was very long and, she admitted, was often more sentimental than practical – such as the small birthday presents made by the children, Albert's cap (NO, that was crossed out and inserted at the top of 'Taking', her mother's sewing box which was a decorative but large and heavy item and not one she had ever used; her own sewing bits and pieces were contained in a large plastic box (and overflowed into one of Dresser's capacious drawers). It was a long list. Possibles.

'Going' - was also long, many large items of furniture which had served them well but would not 'fit' into her new sleek minimal life. Then followed another drink while she mulled over whether sleek and minimal was really achievable, knowing her predilection for collecting – not Major things, not Huge things but rather bits and pieces which appealed and were savoured for their connections with people or places or … Moments. And then there were the Things accrued by the family with diverse interests and activities and then were no longer needed or used but Might Come in Useful. Some of those might yet be claimed, she thought, without much real hope. But one never knew.

It was a busy and happy week, one filled with ideas and thoughts, and purposeful without commitment – for Tommy had reminded her that this was a Quote, nothing definite. Which meant no more doubts or worries as Friday week approached.

Friday dawned grey and misty, undecided. Not at all like Agatha, who was waiting for Shottely and Sons with cheerful anticipation as she loaded the tray with mugs and plates, filled the kettle and put the tins of cakes and biscuits on the table. She had not been so busy for a while. Strong tea, she guessed, they would be big beefy men and was glad she had thought to make some ginger cake. Even if they were not taking anything away that day, they would need to maintain their stamina.

Ten o'clock came and went, she tried not to check the clock ('Going', sadly, but she was hopeful, thought grandfather clocks had a following) and went out to check down the hill for the third time. This time she was rewarded by the sight of a grey car turning in from the road and beginning its ascent to the farm. Agatha wondered who could be coming – another lost tourist blaming the satnav? – before she bethought herself, Shottely and Sons would not need to come in a van on a Quote. She had wondered if all four sons would be accompanying father and told herself, probably not. Realised only then, perhaps only Mr Shottely himself. She had pictured him as a hefty chap, used to manhandling heavy furniture, or perhaps a little stooped by now and very much in charge, ordering his stalwart sons about.

In view of this, it was more than a surprise when the grey car came to a halt on the other side of the low wall and a young man unfolded himself from behind the steering wheel. He was tall, but certainly not stalwart (she had become rather attached to the word 'stalwart')   – in fact the word 'stripling' flashed into her mind before she pulled herself together saying, 'Morning?'

Stripling smiled briefly, turned back into car to retrieve a clipboard and briefcase, turned to smile again, 'Shottely and Sons, Mrs Braithwaite. Good morning.'

Agatha could not stop herself from peering into the back of the car before recollecting herself and unlatching the low gate in the wall, 'Come in, do come in.' Stripling – young man! – held out a card as he stepped through, turned to close it.

'Simon Shottely

Shottely and Sons

Valuations, removals, house clearances'

'Come in, Simon, (it was all first names these days she had learned). So, you are a Son? And would you like a cup of tea or coffee? A little ginger cake? Or a biscuit?'

If she was burbling, he gave no indication.

'It's youngest son actually and tea would be very nice indeed thank you.' And he smiled down at her, then gave the briefest of glances round the kitchen as he placed the clipboard on the table.

It was remarkably easy, almost as if one of Tommy's friends had dropped in. They chatted over the tea and ginger cake almost like old friends about the view and the sensible approach to moving while one was still able to embark upon new changes and possibly new activities. Agatha admitted to a long-held ambition to learn to play mah-jong. Tommy had informed her of small groups and classes in the small market town, whereupon Simon offered the information that his aunt Rebecca was a mah-jong player and seemed to enjoy her weekly game.

They could have chatted for quite a while, but Agatha was determined to be professional as if she were used to moving house and lifestyle regularly and suggested that perhaps Simon might like to make a start. He mentally thanked his father for the advice to let old ladies talk, 'get it out of their system … and they've probably not said a word to another living soul for a couple of days' as he agreed, suggesting they start upstairs and work their way down.

It was all extremely amicable. Agatha guiding him from room to room, standing back to say precisely what she was keeping and Simon making a note of larger items which most definitely Had To Go. There would be boxes of Assorted Small items – probably a lot of that, thought Simon, having toured many old houses. It was still a surprise to him how much Stuff families accumulated.

Finally, they came to rest in the kitchen again, where Simon laid the clipboard on the table with alacrity when Agatha suggested another tea? 'It was very tasty ginger cake,' he hinted, looking around as Agatha busied herself with kettle and mugs and fresh plates. He scribbled more notes as they refreshed themselves. He was at pains by this stage to explain how the market for 'brown furniture' was slow but there was a steady demand for older pieces – 'Some folk like to have an older piece or two – some think it gives the home a feeling of history – an old chair or chest for example, smaller chests of drawers, stools or trunks are used for coffee tables.' He paused, took another bite of cake, chewed thoughtfully.

'Large kitchen tables often do very well,' he added. 'Kitchen diners being popular.'

Agatha nodded, 'Glad to hear that. I couldn't possibly take this with me. But it's been a good family table for a long time - my husband's family had it before us. And probably his grandparents. Quite a bit of the stuff dates back to then.' Nodding at the Dresser, she smiled, 'I suppose *that* will have to be part of fixtures and fittings.'

Simon regarded the Dresser over the rim of his mug.

'Only if you want. They do split in half. Bit of a limited market of course, a piece that size.'

It splits in half, thought Agatha, fancy that! Thought it had been built on the spot and never moved. Well, I've never cleaned under or behind. It comes right down to the floor and backs right up by the wall. Thought it was, well, never to be moved. You live and learn.

'Really? I planned to get rid of it – but it was useful

when the children were small. Don't suppose anyone else would want it.'

She waved him off after a while, clutching the provisional estimate and smiling to herself at the thought of how well the visit had gone and what a very nice young man young Shottely was.

She might have reviewed her opinion if only she could have heard him on his mobile, 'Yes Dad, worth doing - some of the pieces will do well enough – mostly Victorian – useful boxes, chairs, small chests – But! there's one piece – 1750 if it's a day – oak press – she just wants rid of – got that for a song – no, no, course not, didn't let on – kind of thing the Americans want.'

And matters proceeded smoothly; Agatha agreed with Tommy that the quote was about what they had expected so there was no need to call for a second opinion. Shottely and Sons were more than welcome to clear the house once Agatha had located her 'convenient and minimal'. And as this is not a tale to be lengthened by long complications and disasters of any kind, one day in early Autumn saw Agatha shaking her tablecloth out of the kitchen door for the last time. She would miss her sparrows and hoped to attract some of their far- flung cousins ere long.

The folded tablecloth was placed neatly on top of Albert's cap in her basket, standing ready on the kitchen table; Shottely and Sons had agreed a mini move in the final quote and her chosen items had preceded her to number 15 the day before. Tommy was due to pick her up at ten and they would be at number 15 ready for delivery from Bentalls of new beds, armchairs and the latest in TVs. Tommy was to stay two nights, helping her to settle in and, more importantly, get to grips with her first Smart TV.

Agatha did not think herself sentimental but had not wanted to see the house emptied by Shottely and Sons; she preferred to leave it as a home not a shell. Ah, and there was Tommy, turning in at the bottom of the lane. She picked up her jacket and basket, stepped out, turned the key in the lock. Dropped it back through the letter box and went to stand by the garden gate.

Driving away, Tommy chatted cheerfully about his drive down as Agatha fixed her eyes on the road ahead, the basket with Albert's cap companionably by her feet.

Just as they were parking the car on the tiny drive outside number 15, Shottely and Son's van was turning in up the lane to the farm. Tommy was out of the car first, saying 'Welcome to number 15, Mum.' As Agatha joined him and stood for a moment looking round the small close, Tommy opened the car boot, lifted out his bags to deposit by the front door.

'Keys, Mum?'

As Agatha rummaged in her bag for an unfamiliar key ring, the door opened at number 14 and a smiling woman stepped out.

'Hello, you're the new people? I'm Mary, and just saying it's nice to meet you and if you need anything or want to find anything, just ring the bell. But I won't delay you.'

And true to her word, almost before Tommy had explained he was only helping his Mum move in, she had disappeared back inside.

They were still laughing as Tommy filled the kettle and Agatha hung Albert's cap on a peg in the small porch.

Meanwhile, back at the farm, the four Shottely sons were standing in the kitchen watching their father slowly shaking his head as he examined the Dresser. Until finally

'Nay, lad. A shame. But easy done. A marriage is complicated. Take a look here, inside here for starters.

273

See them drawers? Victorian, 1800 or a bit later. Right enough t'cupboard is 1750ish – them panels tells thee straight away. But check the drawers at t'bottom – three short ower two long – should be wi' two short and two false - ower one long – and there's no feet – that should have telled thee first off.'

Simon looked at his feet while his brothers tried to hide their grins.

'Like I said. Easy done. See a lot of these about, marriages. One period with another. And both pieces are oak, which can mislead. Can sell it as one - or two separate pieces more like, not many folk have room for a press these days. Housekeepers' cupboards some folk call 'em. Well, tha's got a cupboard and a set o' drawers but doubt tha'll be mekin' a sale i' States. Now, let's get a move on lads.'

THE RUG WAS OUT OF POSITION

Dulcie inserted the key and turned it slowly.

She always savoured this moment. No matter how long or short, how enjoyable or how predictable the trip – Dulcie was fortunate to have enjoyed a couple of cruises this year - she always keenly anticipated the moment of being Back Home. Even a quick sortie down to the supermarket or round the market at the weekend – the feeling was always the same. A mixture of comfort, relief, relaxation … if asked, she might have said it was akin to taking off a heavy coat or perhaps like slipping on a pair of very comfy slippers.

She opened the door and inhaled deeply – a hint of roses from the FragrantAir capsule she always took care to leave plugged in near the front door – first impressions are So Important she always thought. After a three week cruise the perfume was still the same (albeit with an underlying tone of shut-in stale air) for she took care to leave a FragrantAir capsule in a second socket but on a timer ensuring as the first one emptied, the second would be switched on. Dulcie was a stickler for meticulous detail.

Carefully she wheeled her EasyGo suitcase along the hall to her bedroom – again, thanks to her careful planning, living in a large apartment ensured there were no stairs to carry cases up and down. After James had died, Dulcie had searched patiently for a large apartment on a first floor in a medium sized expensive purpose-built block. First floor and centrally placed, ensured that there were flats above and below and, on each side, – useful insulation against the worst of winter weather. And an expensive block, of course, guaranteed a lift and that the apartments were well sound proofed.

She had disposed of most of the house contents before she sold the house – and did not regret their departure to the auction house one bit. James had inherited a great deal of antique furniture from his parents and grandparents – and had indeed invested in a quite a number of purchases himself. Dulcie had smiled and carefully polished even as she gritted her teeth over the carved wood chests, the endless bars and spindles of old chairs, not to mention, polishing the silver at regular intervals.

Thankfully James had been right, they had all held their value well. He might have regretted their being boxed up for America and the resultant cultural loss to England but Dulcie, seated at the rear of the auction rooms, had kept her mental calculator clicking along as she smiled absently at her catalogue.

Friends said how well Dulcie bore her loss, how brave she was facing each day with a gentle smile. Little did they know that each evening, as the contents of the house were slowly and steadily moving on, she pored over catalogues of streamlined sleek fitted furniture and estate agents' brochures of select apartments in desirable areas as she sipped slowly at a sweet sherry. By the time she was down to the minimum of furnishings, a buyer for the house was confirmed and she had found her new home.

Moving to Ashton had always been part of her plan – a plan she had not shared with her circle of friends. After all, they had been James' friends and although she had been welcomed into the well-established group, she had never felt that she really belonged. She had every intention of carving a new life with a circle of new friends. Ashton was an attractive market town, small enough to be friendly but large enough to have everything she might require. Although comparatively small, Ashton had flourishing and varied activities, well supported by the large number of early retirees, who appreciated the town's history and architecture and its position not too distant from a city with further resources.

EasyGo suitcase deposited neatly on the cream carpet by the wardrobe, she slipped off her shoes and inserted her feet into the pair of fluffy pink slippers by the bed. Dropped her handbag on the chest of drawers and the door keys in the pink china bowl. Slid her jacket off her shoulders and hung it in the wardrobe. And stretched. Stretched and smiled as she gazed at the gleaming white fitted furniture, the cream carpet, the few touches of pink – bedside lamps, delicate pink sprigs of flowers on the cream curtains and the pink dressing gown on the foot of the bed. Not one item of brown furniture.

A lazy evening in front of the TV she promised herself … after a shower.

But first a cup of tea.

Dulcie padded back along the corridor and into the kitchen. Again, the sleek crisp white fittings brought a smile to her face as she filled the kettle with fresh water, set out a tray with white cloth and pink flowered teacup and saucer. Took a meal for one from the freezer and set it on a plate by the microwave. And put four green tea buds in the teapot just before the water boiled.

It was all so perfect; light, sleek and so easy to maintain while the manicured park across the road was a delight to the eye and not one weed was her responsibility. Sighing with satisfaction she carried the tray through the double doors into the lounge diner and set it down on the low coffee table by the window. Cruises were all very well, but she had missed her park. Settled in the Grande Papilio armchair – one could not best Italian design for comfort and elegance she always said - she leaned back to savour the first moments of being truly Back Home.

Picking up the diary on the small table by the chair, she stroked the pink velvet cover reflectively for few moments. No need really to consult the coming week: Mondays to Fridays, each had its allotted activity and group of new acquaintances. Friday evenings and weekends she kept free for special invitations and … opportunities. And sadly, as she very well knew, her weekends had been completely lacking in both since her arrival in Ashton two years ago.

Tea buds slowly uncurling, she poured her first cup of tea. It was frustrating – nay, it was irritating, maddening. Was all her planning in vain? Where were the interesting compatible entertaining friends she deserved and apparently sought in vain? Inhaling the fragrant tea, she mentally reviewed her weekdays, neatly compartmentalised between a church, a charity and six cultural activities and sipped slowly as she wondered whether she had erred or was being too impatient.

Believing Ashton to be her intellectual and cultural haven, Dulcie had embraced each and every opportunity with carefully restrained enthusiasm – one did not wish to become involved in unsuitable relationships or situations from which one would then have to extricate oneself. Oh, she had made … friends … but not friends who invited her more often than was necessary to fulfil a routine - the Book Club was a case in point. Meeting at each other's homes in turn had proved to be – just that. There had been no spontaneous phone call subsequently … no invitation to pop round for a coffee … and when she had, in desperation, issued such a casual 'Care to….?' it had met with a most polite but obvious rebuff.

And her weekends were most definitely quiet. So quiet she had found herself gazing out of the window envying the couples or groups strolling and chatting across the park. She had for a brief moment debated whether to buy a dog – join the dog walkers. But recognising the indisputable fact that a dog could not be hung by the door until the next walk that idea was rapidly abandoned.

Pouring a second cup of tea Dulcie began to wonder

why and how she herself was failing – why did she seem to be making all the approaches? Why were her overtures unreciprocated? Or even rebuffed - in most polite ways, but nevertheless she was turned down. The chilling thought was that … that there was something wrong with her …

She reviewed her modus operandi. Select the ideal area and home. Tick.

Choose suitable and varied activities. Tick.

Be consistently cheerful and cooperative. Tick.

Always listen and make relevant comments. Tick.

Have a fund of amusing anecdotes for the right occasion. Tick.

Volunteer but don't be pushy. Tick.

What more could she do?

Time passed. The remaining tea grew cold. And Dulcie sat on. Wondering why she did not feel truly accepted and part of a group – much less groups.

Beginning to feel a bit chilly, she turned to pick up the cashmere rug from beside her chair.

It was not there.

Which was perfectly absurd.

James had been, in his way, a delightful chap but his casual ways had been most irritating. Things were never in the same place twice. Once moved and settled in her new home, Dulcie had revelled in the fact that everything had its place. And the rug was to the left of her chair so that it could be slipped over her knees as she sat on in the evenings, reading her book or watching TV and occasionally glancing out of the window.

Only it was not there.

The rug was out of its position.

Astounded, she found she was looking again. And again. Double checked.

She stood up and stared down at the small chest. It held library books awaiting return, a spare cushion. And a box of tissues. The rug lay folded on top. Only now it didn't.

She looked round the box, even as she knew that she was being ridiculous. It would have been in full view. Lifting the lid, she looked inside. Even more ridiculous.

For some stupid reason her heart was pounding, making it difficult for her to breathe normally. Her rug had gone! It was not there!

Someone had moved her rug.

Who had been here? Was still here? She stared, wide eyed, round the room, ears strained for sounds, a sound.

But all was silent. Perfectly quiet.

Found she was holding her breath, released it in a gasp, forced herself to breath in. And out. In. And out. All the while listening, ears strained – to hear – the silence.

But was she alone? Was there someone still in her apartment, someone who had moved or taken her rug? She would have to look.

She stared round the room, heart still thumping. There was nowhere for anyone to hide. She could look from the dining area near the kitchen door, and round the rest of the lounge area. Every piece of carefully selected furniture in place and the mystery intruder could not concealed himself in the fitted units.

So, on to the bedrooms. The corridor right angled halfway from the front door to the bedrooms. She approached her bedroom cautiously, tiptoeing in her slippers along the carpet – had he been hiding in her other wardrobe? Should she arm herself? With what? No souvenir knobkerrie or such hung on a convenient wall … she would have to rely on the element of surprise – or appeal to his better nature … Wild ideas jostled for position.

Stepping gingerly through the bedroom door, her eyes lit on her shoes, still on the carpet by the wardrobe door. The small heel could inflict damage if she got her blows in first. Seizing a shoe in her right hand, she approached the second wardrobe, inhaled and flung the door open with her left hand. The winter jackets hung neatly, and she could see below … only her winter shoes.

He had to be in the spare bedroom.

By now images of a scruffy unshaven layabout was being superseded by a haggard wild-eyed teenage druggie and for a moment she thought of running for help. But where? Along the corridor, beating on all the closed doors … would anyone be home? Phone the police? He would hear her and attack before she could even give her address.

No, she had to face this alone. Still armed with the shoe, she slowly depressed the door handle, eased the door ajar, relaxed the handle silently and cautiously opened the door. Deafened by her heart's pounding … and yet she knew the room was silent. Unused by any visitor, the room had an air of - neglect? Oh, it was perfectly clean of course but it carried an air of disuse, neglect, unused. He would be in this wardrobe – plenty of room in an empty wardrobe. Empty except for a spare pillow on the top shelf. Perhaps he was wrapped in her cashmere rug and was sleeping off some drug excess, thinking himself safe from discovery. Well, she would show him. And looking round she spotted the heavy alabaster candlestick on the chest of drawers next to her. Laid the shoe next to it, gripped the candlestick in right hand and advanced on the wardrobe door, flung it open …

And stared at the pillow.

She was almost sick with the anti-climax. Stood quite still as hot flush was followed by cold sweat. There could be no intruder still lurking in her apartment. He had been and gone. Shaking with relief, she went through each room and then returned the candlestick, retrieved her shoe, put it back beside its partner and went automatically into the kitchen and switched on the kettle.

The cup that cheers they say. It wasn't cheering, it was a solution that was needed. For the first time it occurred to her that she was obsessing over the rug – what else was missing? Perhaps he had piled up so much loot, he had carried it away bundled up in the rug. She could see him now, ransacking the place, fingering her precious bits of jewellery, the small silver trinkets she had kept from James' collection – suddenly they were of immense sentimental value. And the useful amount of cash she kept in case … in case of what she had no idea.

Heart pounding again, Dulcie set her cup down on the worktop, frantically thinking where to start first.

Bedroom. Determined to work carefully and systematically, she opened the first drawer…

And some time later she came to a halt back by the kitchen door. Nothing else was missing. Not a single item. Everything was neatly in its place; nothing had been moved. Much less taken. Now what was she to do? Apart from the fact that it had been such a light warm rug, its muted colours had been so pleasing to the eye.

Plus, it had been rather expensive. Very expensive, she mentally adjusted the description realising that she could perhaps make a claim on her household insurance. But first she would have to report it to the police. Not that she expected any practical assistance but from past conversations she was well aware one needed a crime number.

She made a fresh pot of tea and sat down to think the matter over. For how do you explain the theft of a rug – no matter how expensive, from a locked apartment and especially when nothing else was taken? No one else had a spare key.here was no sign of a break in. Would she be believed? But what other explanation was there? And yet she had to admit it sounded most implausible.

A sob rose in her throat – supposing he came back? However he came in, he could do so again. Could he have somehow purloined a key from … a previous owner … the estate agent's office … she would never feel safe here again. Yes, she could put the chain on the door when she was home – but she had to go out – she could not stay home for ever. She would have to change the locks.

The phone rang.

She dropped her cup, tea splashing across the cream

carpet.

Trembling Dulcie stretched her hand out, picked up the phone from the coffee table and croaked, 'Yes?'

'Dulcie? Dulcie Anstruther? Emily Cartwright here. This is a bit of a long shot – we all know how very busy you are – but thought I'd try anyway. A few of us are organising a Christmas Fair for the church – early days and all that – but one has to plan ahead. I wondered if you would care to join us Monday week and perhaps consider being on the organising committee?'

The pause grew as Dulcie frantically tried to drag her mind from cashmere rugs and druggie intruders and focus on the message.

'Are you there? Hello?'

Dulcie coughed, recovered, and managed to make what she fervently hoped was a suitably agreeable response and agreed to the meeting at eleven o'clock in the morning and staying on for lunch. Putting down the phone she could only hope she had not sounded distracted to the point of incoherence.

At last! An actual invitation. And from Emily Cartwright

herself.

Pulling herself together, she picked up the cup, located the spray carpet shampoo. Then prepared herself for a trip to the police station – she could hardly expect a visit. Emily Cartwright and committees swirling together with intruders, Dulcie put on a jacket, picked up her door keys from the bedroom. Walked to the front door to pick up the garage and car keys from the bowl on the small table. Underneath the keys was a slip of paper.

Absently she turned it over -

SELECT LAUNDRY

For Those Special Items

1 cashmere rug

Collection ... *Friday 22 September*

Cost   ...   **£49.99**

How could she have forgotten? As waves of relief swept over her, Dulcie could have cried. Relief was rapidly superseded by a fear. This absolutely foolish forgetfulness … could she possibly be…? … could this be the first signs of dementia?

Then the thought of Emily Cartwright's call helped to calm her down as she firmly sat on the sudden panicky thought. She would deal with that later.

AT THE BOTTOM OF THE STAIRS

Isabel paused. As she always did. And looked up the stairs.

Only nowadays, she reflected, it was more than a pause. It was a halt. A stop. And gird your loins before the ascent.

It hadn't always been like that of course.

She had been conscious from the first time that Philippe had brought her here, to introduce her to his Mama and Papa, that she would be struck, always be aware of the beauty of the stairs before her. The grand double doors, panelled and carved in exquisite detail, had left her unmoved, as had the shallow steps ascending with the backdrop of the charming medieval village. It was the stairs which had caused her to pause, and gaze in appreciation of their perfect symmetry and carefully proportioned balustrades.

She moved the string bag from her left hand to the right,

smiled yet again and took a deep breath. She couldn't help it; she had to smile, had to smile at the beauty of the staircase. Even now with the dried autumn leaves drifting in the corners and fallen plaster lying unswept where it fell on steps and landings, she only saw the beauty of proportion and light and shade.

'Come!' Philippe had said, sweeping an arm out as he flung one of the double doors back and waving carelessly towards the staircase. 'Come and meet Mama and Papa. They will love you and welcome you into our home!'

They hadn't of course, but that was history now.

Mama and Papa would rather Philippe had met and married a nice Catholic French girl – they had, in fact, several possibilities in mind. A long engagement and formal wedding with all the relatives. And all done in the proper traditional family way. They had not anticipated that Philippe would fall in love with a blonde, unknown English girl – a Protestant to boot – and that he would rush her into a whirlwind romance and marriage at the nearest registry office in Brighton, where they had met as students. None of which he had thought to communicate. Perhaps, it could be said in mitigation, that as Isabel was alone in the world and had no need to consult or share, he too had been carried along, unthinking in their shared passion and total self-preoccupation.

As Isabel now began the slow trudge up the steps, the vegetables in the string bag bumping gently against her leg, she recalled the long silence when Philippe had ushered her into the bright salon and cried in ringing tones, 'Mama! Papa! Meet my wife! My beautiful, adorable Isabel!'

It had been an uncomfortable afternoon. Philippe, seemingly unaware of the emotional havoc he had wrought, had chattered on full of their plans alternating with descriptions of their unconventional honeymoon, walking in Scotland, which had extended into Ireland and back via Wales as they photographed and sketched out their ideas for an art centre in the Lake district. For a few years, he added, and then opening up and developing the idea back here in France as they refined the details.

But even he, at last, became aware of the frosty reception and the conversation lapsed into a more intermittent exchange. It had not become any easier. Finally abandoning their plans, Philippe had sulkily, at first, then with apparent resigned acquiescence, settled into the family art business. Moving to and fro, between shops and galleries, son of the owner, heir apparent, it had actually been relatively easy for him Isabel suspected. But not for her. There was no place for her in the existing system. She would stay home – in the family home, be the wife, defer to Mama in all things and produce the family, the next in line. It was a slowly growing realisation of course and she too, had acquiesced before realising it was not what she wanted.

No family back in England, friendships had lapsed, a career had not even been started. How could she go back? And to what? But anyway, she still adored Philippe. Then.

Perhaps it would all have been much easier if the family had come along as expected. If she could have, she would have. But time passed, medical opinions and advice were sought. It was not to be. Philippe could not produce an heir. Terribly sad, a tragedy really. And made all the worse by the fact that Isabel knew that somehow his parents still blamed her. It was all her fault.

For a while Philippe sought consolation – Isabel suspected he sought an heir – debated how she would react and respond if faced with a bastard heir. Would she, could she accept an adoption? An official solution? But of course, it did not, could not happen. She tried not to allow the word 'fault' into her conscious thoughts. It was how it was. They talked about it of course, in the early days. She waited hugging her despair, while he chased his phantoms, knowing he would come back to her.

And life moved on. Living in the family home. And in Mama's unchanging routine.

In some strange way that she could not explain, nor did she attempt to do so, she was consoled, comforted by the staircase. How can you explain or understand how something so silent and inanimate can be a comfort? But it was so. The days when Philippe's absence – 'checking a gallery opening '– was extended and he could not be easily reached by phone, she tried not to think what he was doing, much less with whom. She would find herself making an excuse for yet another walk; a slow soothing walk down and later, back up the staircase.

She would anticipate his return, always faintly regretful – for he knew she knew – and knew how his face would brighten, seeing her coming down to meet him. They would hug, on the stairs, he would hold her close, and she would listen to his heartbeat. They would walk up slowly, arms wrapped closely round each other. He would pause, look down and kiss her yet again. And she knew he was hers. Always.

How do you mark time? The seasons? There were no

children to watch, moving from the first staggering steps to the joyous racing in carefree childhood, no teenagers to help through the agonies of first relationships.

Isabel marked the time in stages, with no clear definitions. There was At the Beginning. And then there was Waiting – waiting for the children who never came, waiting for his parents to accept her. There was the seemingly endless Managing – managing to keep cheerful and hopeful when Philippe pursued his fantasy. Almost easier was the Caring – for his parents, who grudgingly accepted her help and assistance as their frailties increased. There was the Together Still – when they were at last alone to feel free, free from the pressure of expectations and disappointments. Finally, there was the Alone.

After Philippe died, she stayed on. For where would she go? And what would she do?

They had talked – briefly – of that long ago dream as his parents aged and the business was under Philippe's control. The art centre which never was. The spark, the enthusiasm, all had faded; it was almost impossible to recall how they had felt and how they had had a vision. Caring for his parents had taken time and energy, a time finally rewarded by their appreciation after so many years.

And after that, when they could no longer share news of developments and events, cause his mother's eyes to widen in amazement, his father's eyes glow with pride, then there was less meaning. Less desire. So easy to let things drift before selling out to a rival. For there was no one to pass it on to.

They had stayed on together, in the house far too large, perched on the hilltop in the centre of the small medieval village, much of which now was sold out as second homes to the distant rich, who might visit occasionally or rent out a house or two for some TV drama. A few locals stayed on; most of their offspring attracted to jobs among the bright lights of some city pulsing with excitement such as Castelsagratt never had. Not since the early fourteenth century anyway.

They were companionably content, in silent agreement never to broach the 'might have beens'. There was enough money - their needs were increasingly simple – but it was easy to defer decisions. And so the house, already old, continued with its decay unchecked, uncared for. Rooms were closed, never to be reopened nor used. For what was the point? When a section of delicately wrought iron balustrade came loose and fell, it was propped by a nearby wall – to be put back 'one day'. As cleaners and gardeners, any workers, aged and left, they were not replaced. Until they were down to Charlotta, who came once a week and wielded a brush and cloth in a desultory manner.

While Philippe was still alive, they would wake early and watch the sun's rays casting its first glow over the tiled roofs, highlighting the quirky angles and shadows. Then down to the kitchen where Isabel would make fresh coffee while Philippe walked to the boulangerie for two baguettes. They would make a simple breakfast together in the kitchen and then repair to the salon, where they would browse over daily papers and watch the leisurely street below. Isabel would make a soup to accompany left over baguette. The afternoons were for a siesta before a stroll together to the old walls, from where they could gaze across the countryside with its tranquil fields and woods.

Back via the church, a pause to gaze again at the stone marking Mama and Papa's final resting place. All punctuated by the occasional greeting from some other aged making his or her perambulation. And then home, for a simple evening meal.

But now Philippe was gone; even less incentive to prepare a simple meal. Isabel lived mostly on soups and rolls, fruit and cheese. It seemed to sustain her very well. She had her daily walk to the boulangerie and was content to sit in quiet contemplation of the street and market square below. Her one joy, if asked, she would have said was her return home and seeing the staircase with its sweeping welcome.

I STILLED MY BREATH
AND REACHED OUT

The wind was cold. To be expected so early in the morning. Leaning on the car, I watched the grey waters rippling smoothly with the tide and felt a small glow of self-satisfaction. No one else had made such an early start and I had it all to myself.

The tide was going out and very soon the causeway would be clear. Already I could make out the roadway, the markers dark and stark in the morning light. It would be safe enough to start driving but being alone made me rather cautious. There were left-behind pools of sea water on the road, the tide still lapped at the causeway edges. I would give it a few more minutes.

It was different this time. We had come in early summer, sunlight sparkling on the waters and the island dramatically before us, filled with promise. A long-held desire to visit Lindisfarne fulfilled at last, the mood had been cheerfully anticipatory. Perhaps in part due to retirement – each and every expedition, event we had enjoyed, reminded us how fortunate we were. Not for us, jetting round the world, no madly expensive exotic cruise. We had trundled through life together accepting life would have its ups and downs but recognising we both had the ability to enjoy life – often the most simple things And we had.

The waters were lower. I got back in the car, shivering slightly against the wind, and started the engine. The car moving slowly forward on to the causeway, the wheels splashing in the rutted pools. Glancing behind, revealed a deserted road and I felt again that glow of achievement. Silly really. We had managed to arrive alone on the causeway, and I'd wanted to repeat that feeling of … of what? Daredevil bravado? It was quite safe if you follow the rules – and yet it felt excitingly different and rather adventurous. Perhaps I'd lived a sheltered life!

'I've done it, Bill,' I said aloud. 'First here and all alone on the crossing.'

Driving carefully, I traversed the causeway, enjoying the grey waters lapping closely on each side and drove up the slight incline on to the island. The feeling of anti-climax took me by surprise and moving on to a convenient place to park, I paused, then parked.

What now?

Bill's death, so abrupt and unexpected, meant I'd focussed on coping, managing, taking the next step. We'd been a bit short of family but had good friends, who had rallied round, and I'd been grateful. Life moved on, inexorably as it does, and the summer had taken me with it. Weeding the flower beds which had been his pride and joy. Carefully nurturing the vegetable garden where he'd spent many contented hours in retirement, I'd kept busy. Found comfort in the garden; the end of summer suddenly set in motion a desire to get away, have a change and out of the blue came a wish to retrace the steps of our last holiday together. I would recall how happy and contented we had been. Enjoy the scenery and check out the places where we had paused. Relive that time.

Only now I was here, it wasn't … wasn't right. Of course, I hadn't been stupid enough to think it would be all the same – no Bill for starters. No Bill. My heart cried loud and long, and I let my head rest on the steering wheel.

No Bill.

Drew a long shuddering breath, for the first time I wanted to howl - like a wolf at the moon – wanted to beat my breast and thump someone, something, with my clenched fists.

Of course, I didn't. One doesn't do that sort of thing. Sat up, looked round, wiped my eyes as I decided what to do next. Thought I'd drive a bit further. And parked again. Having arrived with departure of the tide in the early dawn, there was no one else about and probably nowhere open. That thought had not occurred to me before.

We had arrived early last time – but the sun had been sparkling on the water, warm on our faces even at that early hour – and we had had each other. We had ambled about, to and fro, Bill clutching the booklet and reading out bits and pieces. We hadn't needed anyone else.

The tourist season dwindles in the autumn but hotels, cafes etc continue to hope and cater for last minute visitors. And so it was, with great relief, I saw the hotel doors being propped open and a chap in shirtsleeves, adjust an awning, yawning as he did so.

I would have breakfast.

A sensible decision, having left the small BnB before the owners were afoot, and I slowly made my way across the cobbled parking area. Shirtsleeves was laying out a series of newspapers along a counter, looking up as I entered.

'Breakfast?' I enquired, smiling.

He cocked a thumb towards a nearby door from which came sounds of cutlery and quiet movement.

'Be the first,' he murmured, slapping down three copies of the Daily Mail.

Taking the precaution of acquiring a paper – The Times – I had something to occupy my mind while I waited for a full English. Breakfast was satisfyingly hot, and I'd reached the toast stage before I was joined by, first, a very young couple who looked as though they should be in school uniform and who whispered, heads lowered. And then a second couple who clearly did not enjoy early morning and retired behind their respective newspapers, a hand reaching out occasionally for more toast or tea. Next a couple with teenage son, clearly bored beyond belief at being expected to breakfast together. His mother hissed that they'd paid for it and if he ate up, lunch could be dispensed with. I suspected it would be anyway.

Apart from a cursory glance over at me, social interaction there was none. But I was finished, had had enough. And as I paid the bill, the realisation hit me – that I'd had enough of Lindisfarne too. I'd seen it all, all that I wanted to, seen it with Bill. He wouldn't be there to share a quote from the booklet, point out some seals, ask what I thought of the line of upturned fishing boats. I might as well leave.

So, as a feeble sun tried to break through the grey clouds I got back in my car and turned its nose back towards the causeway. There was plenty of time before the tide came in again – and what would I do if I stayed? I'd move on.

What else had we enjoyed? Bamburgh Castle – now that had been fascinating. Photos were banned in the castle, and I'd been frustrated, seeing angles and corners I would have liked to sketch. Could have sketched from photos – pausing to draw on the guided tour clearly wasn't an option. I could go on there, try a sneaky photo or two when the guide was diverted, and my car headed south.

The sun was making a more determined effort, Bamburgh made an impressive outline against the sky. But first I would pay a visit to the garden; Bill had waxed lyrical at Gertrud Jekyll's work – I would take a few more photos. We had envied the walled garden, dreamed of one day … knowing it was a dream but enjoying it all the same. Now Autumn had arrived, pathways littered with leaves, flower beds straggling and an overall atmosphere of end-of-the-day, time to close down and sleep.

I wished I hadn't come. The sneaky photo shoot in the castle lost all appeal.

Odd, that I had had the sense not to rebook in Ford. We had found Lady Waterford Hall most intriguing, and I had recognised it very much as a one-off. So, I'd spent the previous night in a small pub. Should have applied that to Lindisfarne and Bamburgh. I'd press on – as I'd planned – across country through Coldstream towards Lauder and the Southern Upland Way.

Bill had suggested we come back one day and walk – at least part – of the Way. I would do that now in his memory. Lindisfarne and Bamburgh would forever remain linked with Bill.

The A697 was well maintained and was a pleasant drive across deserted countryside – would have been even better in bright sunshine, it was beginning to cloud over again, but at least it wasn't raining. Coldstream then Greenlaw and on to Lauder; the tiny hamlets of Houndslow and Whiteburn barely discernible. I was in no hurry. Lauder would do very nicely for lunch – a small one, I thought, smiling at the memory of the teenager being exhorted to eat a hearty breakfast.

It proved to be market day, so I munched on a sausage roll as I wandered round a few stalls. Stopped for a coffee at another stall and exchanged a few pleasantries with the woman as she washed a few mugs in a bowl in her van.

The Southern Upland Way ran through Lauder in a convenient manner. I would leave the car at the edge of the marketplace and walk a few miles, take a few photos and talk with Bill. I did this often. Told him what I was thinking, asked what he thought. Looking at the map, I saw the Way went through Edgarhope Wood, which would be a nice change from the wide bare expanses, and then on to Scoured Rig, perhaps I'd walk as far as Watch Water reservoir? There were no indications of any buildings, habitations, farms but Longformacus was only a few miles past the reservoir. Bound to be a small caff … and if not, or if I turned back earlier, I had my rucksack. A bottle of water and a couple of Kitkats and an apple were more than enough for an afternoon's ramble. Less than sixteen miles by my calculations.

Changed into walking boots, hoisted the rucksack on my shoulders after checking a waterproof was safely stowed inside and off I went. When Bill insisted that I wear proper walking boots all those years ago, I'd initially resented it but by the end of our first long walk, I'd admitted how right he was. As he had been about so many things. It felt good to be striding along breathing in the fresh air and remembering how we'd smile at each other at the first squirrel, the first buzzard, the first fly agaric ... all the firsts each time we set off.

Edgarhope Wood wasn't what I'd hoped for, and I admitted that was my fault. Suppose I was in the mood for a lowland oak forest with ancient trees – not this coniferous stretch. No matter. It was trees, reaching up to sweep the sky – well, clouds. Couldn't even be a bit poetic. And it didn't last for too long; I was soon out onto the track winding its way up to – what was it, checked the map ... I would have checked the map but saw it now, mentally, resting on the passenger seat as I laced my boots.

Edgarhope Wood then ...something Rig, something to do with scrubbing ... Scoured Rig ... it was there on the leaning post, indicating a slight turn to the left. Wondered if the post was leaning from the prevailing winds – it must fairly howl across here in the winters I thought. My boots crunched satisfactorily on the patches of gravel but for the most part the track was muddy beaten earth. On both sides the land fell away, disappearing into a cloudy haze. I was walking slightly uphill now but with no clearly defined summit. Small streams trickled alongside, disappeared under the track, their whispering chatter a quiet accompaniment.

Another post came into view. 'Hunt Law 1625' was neatly inscribed. I paused. Must be higher than where I am, wonder if I'd get a good view – a sort of wide-angle vista? Looked at my watch. There was plenty of time and anyway, nothing was set in stone. I could follow the sign, get my photo and if it took a bit longer than expected, - why, I could just walk back down into Lauder. I'd yet to find a place for the night.

Watery sunlight lit the path ahead to Hunt Law - an omen for a good picture? I set off.

More uphill walking but only to be expected if I were to stand on top of some hill. You'd love this Bill, wouldn't you? Only us in the world, you'd say, and go off in some fantasy of civilisation being wiped out, we are the only survivors, and start making plans about how we would emulate Robinson Crusoe. Do you remember the time I said, if that's the case I'm not washing up anymore. You stood still and stared. Then laughed when I said there will be more than enough crockery in the world … said I had a strange set of priorities.

There was a bit of a wind getting up, pulled the zip up

on my fleece, glad I'd thought to bring a woolly hat. It couldn't be far now, paused to look around. I'd been focussing on the track ahead, one boot in front of the other. Wide bare expanses of scrubby grass, thin low bushes scattered about and a complete lack of habitation – precious few trees too. This would be a picture to remember. All this nothing much stretching on and on.

Another sign, indicating a track to the right, even thinner than this one. Meikle Says Law 1755. Higher still! Should I? pulled my sleeve back, no, Hunt Law will have to do. I've yet to find a bed for the night. Pity. Plodded on. And spotted what must be Hunt Law sign on the horizon, not far now and I Have Done It. Bill said I talked in capitals at times.

Yes! I've done it. Hunt Law, 1625 and now a selfie with the post.

Sat on the grass to gaze around. And a swig of water. And a Kitkat, crinkling the foil into a small ball to drop in the rucksack. Success! I've done a walk by myself – you are still with me, but I've done this myself. You know what I mean. Flipped the photos back on my phone, there you are at Lindisfarne. And us at Bamburgh. Oh, we had a lovely time, didn't we? Flipped a few more pictures, smiling as a few tears dripped. Wiped my eyes and stood up, slipping the phone into my pocket. Looked back the way I'd come.

And saw the curls of low mist – cloud? Curling across the moor towards me. Good job I got here and its only downhill most of the way back. I set off.

It's a funny thing, I've noticed it before. You think walking uphill would be harder than downhill. It's not. I read recently even walking downstairs uses more calories than walking upstairs – something to do with the pressure or tension on muscles. I think.

Whatever it was, it was slower walking down, watching the track carefully as it twisted along, and being grateful for the boots' support when awkward stones tripped my unwary ankles. I'd walk as far as the Rig, that sharp escarpment bit and have the second Kitkat. It was definitely slower coming down. I glanced up to see how far to the post and was surprised to see mist covering the way in a soft gentle blanket. Could not see the post. Felt a momentary clutch of panic before I reminded myself that as I neared it, so I would see through the mist better. Only a bit of low-lying cloud after all. Walked on, the rattle of gravel against my boots the only sound.

I was walking in mist now. It was like walking in steam

and I smiled thinking of a sauna we'd once tried. But then, looking up, realised it was thicker and darker as if the light were fading. But it was OK, I was on the track which led all the way back to Lauder - well, to the tarmac road at the edge of Lauder.

Strange.

That was one enormous boulder, nearly tripped as I passed close by it. Boulder. There had been no boulder on the path. There is now. How come I didn't see it before? Paused, looked round, was there anything familiar? Turned to go on. And stood still. Which way had I been facing?

Now I did admit to a faint feeling of fear. Calm down, take a deep breath. Now, down on the track. This is the track? It looks like anywhere.

Face and hair wet with mist and heart thudding faster than the boots. I must keep going down. Back to Lauder. Took the phone out of my pocket and felt alarm at the 20%. I hadn't spent too long looking at the photos and only took a few. But had I charged it last night?

Never mind. Keep on going. I was stumbling now, trying to hurry and trying not to admit I wasn't sure if I was actually on the track. Sometimes it looked familiar. Then it didn't. But I couldn't go back, must keep going on. The dark damp silence pressed around me.

It seemed for ever. Stumbling on. Getting nowhere. On track. Off track. What track?

A huge dark shape loomed in the gloom. A house?! I must have stumbled on a farm track. Oh Bill, where am I? There wasn't a house coming up was there? Not a house. An outbuilding of some sort. Would I be sleeping with the cows? Would there be shelter? Just a blank wall. Felt my way along the rough wood and round a corner, and along, and another corner. And a door. I banged. My frozen fingers fumbled for a latch until miraculously the door creaked half open. Stumbling in, arms stretched out, there was a faint square of light opposite and as I lurched towards it, crashed into something solid. The abruptness of it made me stop. Stop dead. Pause. Slowed my ragged panting breath. I could hear Bill, Slow down, love, slow down.

I stilled my breath and reached out, something flat and solid. Remembered phone. Held it up and reached out, the faint light revealed a table. On which was a candlestick. A candle. A box of matches.

Bothies are shelters, very often old buildings made of stone or wood with basic facilities like a real fire and cooker if you're lucky. Found in remote areas these are free to stay in and mainly used by hillwalkers.

Bill was always reading out bits from the booklets and leaflets he picked up. I could shelter here, wait for the mist to clear. Or until the morning.

LETTER FOR BENJIE

High Meadow

12th August 1960

My dear Benjie,

I was always going to write this letter because I knew I would find it hard to tell you in so many words face to face. I have written it in my head so many times. Only of course, the time has come too soon. I always planned to write it for you after your twenty first birthday. Then you would be a man and whatever you chose to do, I hoped and believed you would be man enough.

But here we are, at a crossroads.

High Meadows has been our home for as long as you can remember – you can't remember coming here, a babe in arms as they say. But true. You were.

I know you faintly remember Nanny; you were six years

317

old when she died and for a long time you would expect her to come home. Understanding the permanence of death is too much for a child to comprehend and I thought at the time, if you believed she was out shopping or visiting a friend and would come home, in time you would accept her absence. And so it was. And we managed to carry on very well on our own. There were many homes without a father in those days after the war.

But Benjie, there are things you could not remember and which we never explained to you. The time was never right and so on. And if I am to be honest – and I must be completely honest now - now that the truth is to be told. I dreaded this day.

Where to begin? Are you sitting comfortably as they used to say on the radio show 'Listen With Mother.' And we used to, didn't we? I wonder if you remember sitting on my lap, Listening With Mother? so long ago.

This is going to take a long time, so you had better – be sitting comfortably I mean. Hope you have made yourself a drink and one of those cheese sandwiches you like. Mr Ravenor is going to give you this after the funeral, hope it all went well. I did try to think of everything to make it easier for you and the McFaddyens next door will have been a great help. Poor Sally couldn't stop crying when I told her, but Jack was a rock as always.

No one can plan for everything of course; I've done my best. Believe me.

When Dr Murphy explained how there was no hope and time was very short, I knew I must get organised to help you.

Mr Ravenor will have explained again how High Meadow belongs to you and that there is money in the bank. I did explain all this to you, but I realised it was very hard for you to believe and understand I wouldn't be here much longer. When you have any problems – and you will have – everyone has problems – go to the McFaddyens next door and if they can't help, go to Mr Ravenor. They will look after your best interests.

Now the next part is between you and me and what you choose to do with it and if you do decide to share it, then that is all up to you. Just please believe we did what we thought best at the time. And after.

We – Mother and I – used to live in Dorset long ago. My father died when I was in my twenties and I stayed on at home, living with Mother and teaching at a primary school nearby. People didn't leave home and have their own flats etc like they do now, so that was all quite usual. And when the war came it made life much easier, having someone to share all the problems with - and there were problems. It was easier in a small town, and we were so very glad we didn't live in a big town or city – they were bombed often.

In fact, it was so quiet where we were that a small orphanage was relocated out of London and into a large house on the edge of town; the owners had gone to America and left instructions it could be rented out. Rented or requisitioned, I don't know. All we knew is that one week it was standing empty and the next week a couple and about twenty children had moved in. It wasn't safe in London, but they found it very difficult adjusting to a small town at first. They were used to better public transport and many shops and deliveries for everything. But they managed and I felt a bit sorry for them, I think we all did. So many children and all under the age of four.

I went there one day and offered to go every weekend for a couple of hours and tell the children stories, have a bit of a sing song. The couple were very grateful, I don't suppose they had much time for that sort of thing. And the children seemed to like having another grown up to listen to; I would tell a story and then we'd talk about it and act some of the parts and I would try to have a song in mind which would link to the story. We could always sing Nursery Rhymes otherwise.

Why am I telling you all this? Because it was a happy time in its way, I did like helping. And it's a bit difficult getting to the point of all this. I think there is a phrase called Setting the Scene. I went one weekend; it was Spring and the weather was bright and sunny and there were primroses on the roadside as I walked along the lane. War seemed very far away.

When I got to the Home, as we called it, Daphne came to the door looking all flustered and as I took off my coat, she started telling me how the director of the charity had arrived that morning with a baby. 'A baby,' she said, 'We never have babies, they are kept in a nursery until they are eighteen months and then move on to the Homes. But things are so difficult in London, this baby was left on a church doorstep last week and they are busy moving the nursery out into the country but…' she started telling me the buts and I forget them.

It all boiled down to the fact that she and her husband had never had a baby before and it was making life almost impossible, it need so much attention. I began to feel very sorry for this poor baby, an It without a name seemingly. However, it meant that I was more than welcome to entertain the toddlers and give her time 'to sort things'.

At the end of the afternoon when the children went to have their tea, I sat with Daphne in the small sitting room to have a cup of tea too. The baby was there, a quiet little thing wrapped in a knitted blanket and lying in a drawer on the floor.

'Not even a cot,' exclaimed Daphne. 'I daresay life is hard back in London but to arrive without warning and dump a baby on us and it hasn't anything to its name except a couple of gowns and a few nappies. And no cot! I tell you, Alison, life is getting almost more than I can bear right now.'

I drank my tea and watched the baby, it just lay there looking at nothing, not making a sound.

I asked if it were a boy or girl and its name? but all she could tell me was it was boy, and no one had thought more than to call it Baby John as it had been found on the steps of St John the Baptist in Clerkenwell. It had been wrapped in the knitted blanket. A sort of patchwork of knitted squares. And suddenly, on the spur of the moment, I heard myself saying, 'Would you like me to take it home with me for the weekend? I'm sure Mother and I can manage for a couple of days, give you time to sort things out.' And to my astonishment she leapt at the offer, bustled off to put the nappies and a spare gown into a bag and before I could think further, I was on the doorstep saying goodbye, Baby John in the crook of my left arm and the bag in my right hand.

You should have seen my mother's face when I walked up the path to the front door, she was looking out of the window as she often did when she expected me home. But to give her her due, she was all sympathy and kindness. Baby John was made all comfy on the sofa with cushions piled around him, although I doubt he could have rolled off at that age. Daphne had given me a box of baby milk powder so we could make a feed, and a bottle.

And that is when I discovered that my mother had kept so many of my baby things up in the attic. The box was brought down and out came my baby nightgowns and bonnets and nappies and first small jumpers and so on. I must have looked very surprised, Mother said she had always thought they would come in useful. By which I suppose she meant she was hoping for a grandchild one day. Well, the war hadn't made that easy with so few men about.

Baby John was very easy to look after. He was bathed in the sink and dressed in some of my baby clothes. He had a bottle of milk and drifted off to sleep on my mother's lap while I made the supper, washed up and eventually we made our way to bed. Baby John sleeping in the basket work crib – brought down from the attic – beside my bed.

But not for long. The drone of planes woke us, German bombers on their way to Portsmouth we thought. Sometime later I heard them again, wondered how much damage had been done when there was an almighty roar and explosion. Afterwards it was agreed they must have had to leave the area and off-loaded a bomb on the way home. We certainly could not have been a target. All they wanted to do was jettison the bomb, lighten the load and so on.

There was no sleep after that, we could see flames in the distance, people running down the road. Normally we both would have gone out, but we had Baby John, so in the end I left my mother and walked down the road to see if there had been any damage. Fortunately, it was at the edge of town, people said. There were people walking to and fro in the moonlight asking for news, wondering what to do. This was part of the war we hadn't experienced.

Fortunately - on the edge of town. Unfortunately - the Home had had a direct hit.

Oh Benjie, what were we to do? We couldn't take you back. We thought we should inform the police – but where would they take Baby John? I couldn't remember much detail about the charity – but someone would have some information somewhere, wouldn't they? Someone from the charity would come down to inspect, to record the damage, the tragedy. And that's when the thought occurred to us, we could look after Baby John until someone came down from London. They would know what to do.

The following week the town hummed with the tragic story, so many small children escaping war torn London only to be bombed in their beds out in the country. We lived down a long lane and during that week had no visitors as usual. And somehow over the long evenings, sitting listening to the radio, taking turns to nurse Baby John we began to think, to wonder if, perhaps, supposing … all manner of things. The gist of it all was that we decided that it would take a lot of effort to trace where Baby John should go – and we certainly didn't think he should go back to London right then. We thought we could keep him and look after him and wait and see, wait until anyone came making enquiries. Especially enquiries for an unnamed baby with no known parents. But no one ever came down from the charity.

There had been reports in the local paper about the Home being bombed but apart from agreeing it was a tragedy no one appeared to be interested. I suppose it was just one more sad event during 1942.

One evening my mother said, 'I suppose we could offer to adopt him, give him a proper home.' And the more we thought about it, the more we realised that we had put ourselves into 'a bit of a pickle' as my mother described it. We had not reported the baby, no one knew he was with us. Why hadn't we? And finally, we had to admit it. We loved that little baby, we wanted to keep him. After all, said my mother, growing up in some orphanage, what chance does he have? We could give him a good start in life.

So, we did, Benjie. We gave you the best start in life we could.

Yes Benjie, Baby John. We could not bear to part with you, we loved you from that first night and wanted to care for you. Forgive us if we did wrong.

Once the decision was made, we had to carefully plan,

we had to be able to explain your presence. We could not keep you a secret, not for long anyway. So, you were explained as a cousin's son left with us while she was busy with important war work in London, husband away at sea.

Friends and neighbours never questioned it, rallied round with some outgrown bits and pieces, rationing was always a problem. And everything was made so much easier when Uncle Jack died and left us High Meadow here in Somerset. No one was surprised when we gave up our rented cottage and made the move into our own home. Jobs were easy come by - it was still war time. We arrived in a village near the market town Taunton, hinted I was a war widow and people either believed that or thought I was an 'unfortunate' single mother. There were many of those.

And so that is the story, Benjie.

We had planned when you were twenty-one to tell you all. I went to London once, went to find St Johns in Clerkenwell, thought there might be some records at the church or at the priest's home – but again, another bombing raid had destroyed them too. We left it there. Did not know how we could find out anymore.

You are now eighteen, I am so glad we had your birthday party with all your friends. You have done well at school. You have a place in college. You can do as much with your life as you want and I'm sure you will be sure to make mum and me proud.

I hope you will forgive us for deciding your future as we did.

Your two gowns and the knitted blanket are in the wooden box, the one we kept locked in the attic.

I wish we could have done more.

With all my love, Mum xxxxx

RED RIBBON

It was coming to the end of my mother-in-law's visit – every three years she would undertake the arduous journey by bus – down through the Northern Province from Lake Bangweleu, across the Congo pedicle and back over the border into Zambia. An uncomfortable journey of over 450 kilometres on crowded buses and queueing at roadblocks, where unpaid Congolese soldiers were trigger happy and were prone to demand a bonsela (a gift).

Widowed and probably in her late 70's or early 80's (African births were not registered long ago so the family had based their calculations on the fact that father-in-law had been able to remember the first missionaries in the area – early 1900's).

Mother-in-law was a force to be reckoned with. No bonselas for the soldiers, but she always brought me a gift. One year a bag of wild rice from her garden, this year a whole hand of bananas from her trees. Her name was Mwape but she was always respectfully called

BaMayo – meaning mother – grandmother. Her English consisted of OK! Or OK? And as my Bemba was sadly limited our shopping expeditions were always hilarious.

She would make what were clearly disparaging comments on goods in the 'European' shops on Cairo Road, our main street in Lusaka. And after a while we would repair to Limbada's on Freedom Way in what had been the second-class trading area. Limbada's was an Indian store – more of a warehouse really – and goods of every description known to man were stacked floor to ceiling. It was an Aladdin's cave – it had everything – it had the unexpected, the unexplained, the wanted and unwanted and all at bargain prices.

But Grandmother knew what she wanted. A pair of takkies (plimsolls – the only footwear which would accommodate her feet spread wide by seventy years of walking barefoot). Two lengths of citenge (traditional prints worn sarong style). Offered anything else, she merely shook her head. She needed nothing more. Then I saw her looking longingly at a stack of brightly coloured plastic pails, so she accepted one with a show of reluctance. But I saw her stroking it with a quiet smile as we put the takkies and citenge into it.

On the way to the exit, I stopped at the children's section

and suggested balls and small dolls with my limited vocabulary. She refused but I managed to squeeze a few in the pail. I knew that the children in the village would look for her return from the city. And then I saw piles of hair ribbon, thought of little girls as their mothers plaited their hair and bought a few metres of bright red ribbon to add to the pail.

Grandmother was completely mystified but I managed to steer her to the exit and through the complicated paying process. (And if you are ever in Lusaka, I urge you to spend some time in Limbada's – the paying and wrapping is an entertainment in itself).

Back home Grandmother spent a happy time looking at her purchases, trying them on, rewrapping them, shaking her head at my extravagance over the balls and dolls. And at long last, when my husband came home, the hair ribbon for little girls was explained. There was much head shaking and 'A-a-as' over my indulgence but into the pail it all went.

Grandmother slept in the guest room off the courtyard – she liked the privacy and could also venture out into the garden with the dogs early in the morning. As it was her last night, I thought suddenly to take her a tray of tea and biscuits. She didn't hear my tap at the door …

so I was treated to Grandmother gazing at herself in the mirror and smiling at the bright red ribbon bow on her hair.

LAGER LADY

Once walking, legs in motion, I was glad I'd set off. Am the first to admit I've never been terribly physical; no jolly hockey sticks back in the far-off teen-age years, I much preferred to hide in some remote corner with a book. It used to amuse me, reading the games mistress' report at the end of each term. She clearly had no idea who I was and 'Fair' and 'Useful member of team' and 'Jane has worked well' followed each other with monotonous regularity.

But this is different. Having agreed to house-sit a friend's dog for three months (she lived almost on the beach, and it was a cheap and cheerful holiday) I had discovered to my amazement that a daily walk was actually enjoyable. Once I had set off. That was the difficult bit. But the dog had to be walked; after that it pottered about the small garden and was no trouble at all and I very soon learned the value of getting out there with it before breakfast. We would have the beach almost to ourselves – there were a few other dog lovers (not that I was) out there, determinedly striding forth, cheerfully calling to their charges and throwing balls and generally indulging in other 'look at me being physical' activities.

Not so Bernard and I (yes, Bernard). Avoiding his reproachful gaze for as long as I could, I would at last capitulate, pick up lead and we would set off. Note, he never wore the lead; we agreed early on in our relationship that it was demeaning to be tethered and under my control. He trotted calmly on my left-hand side, next to the casually swinging lead, until we reached the corner where he would halt, assume a thoughtful air, turn round five times and deposit the first bowel movement of the day. I would neatly package it up, deposit it in nearby dog bin and we would move on, agreeing it had never happened and was nothing to do with us. In a few more minutes we were on the beach whereupon he would make various investigations in my vicinity, never wandering too far from my route along the beach as far as the rock fall and back again and completely ignoring any overture from a passing canine – and its walker.

We got on very well, Bernard and I, both loners with little interest in casual would be acquaintances.

This is a long preamble - just explaining how I came to appreciate the value of a daily walk. We would both return, refreshed and filled with a pleasant quiet energy.

Bernard would fill his day then with naps interspersed with investigations in flower beds and the dusty, subterranean bowels of the three laurel bushes. I would complete a whirlwind clean-and-tidy-up before establishing myself on the patio with laptop and coffee and a succession of toasted bagels and apples.

It was a most enjoyable and profitable holiday. Bernard was fit and well. Friend was forever indebted. And I finished the novel which had been the bane of my life all the previous winter and my agent no longer avoided me.

And I am left with the need for a morning walk.

Once back home I slipped into my usual slothful ways, but only for a few days. Could not concentrate, could not settle down until it dawned on me that I was missing my walk. No, I did not rush out and get myself a dog. Nothing so rash. But I do now walk round the block every morning. Am the first to admit that primarily it is to quell the uneasy guilt feeling which swamps my ability to think clearly and constructively until I've had my Daily Exercise – elevated with capital letters to denote its permanence in my life.

Sadly, no beach within reach – am not going to drive somewhere to have a walk!! So, I walk along three residential streets, divert through a park and then a zigzag via more residential streets back home. It serves its purpose.

This morning was very much as usual. Walked early as is my wont – far less likely to meet a neighbour (I am on nodding terms with a few) or sweating joggers, who cannot divert from their set path even if it is directly across mine, and so on. The streets were empty, children had gone or been escorted to their place of learning, parents had gone to work or returned from the school run to reward self with coffee and a bit of TV. Number 26 sported a new For Sale board. The rusty car outside number 44 had been towed away – or more likely loaded onto some breakdown truck. Whichever, the old chap, with the fair isle sweater, would be happy – he had felt it incumbent upon himself to pause, shears in hand, and explain over the hedge that the car was nothing to do with him and the Council was slow to act despite his phoning every Monday morning. I sympathised.

Turned into the park and walked under the trees admiring the pattern of leaves against the blue of the sky and the squirrels making merry among the branches. Walk later, and the park would be heaving with teenage couples walking hand in hand, wires dangling from ears, oblivious of other pedestrians on the same path and the shrieks of children dangling from various sections of play equipment as their parents smoked and compared notes or called admonishment and advice to their Gary, Melissa, Charlie or Traceeeee.

Early morning had many advantages.

And today I was not the only one. Someone was sitting on the bench beside the path as I neared the end of the park. I became uncomfortably aware that I was being watched. Used to hate that when I was a young teenager, walking along a street faced with oncoming pedestrian, who I was sure was analysing my clothes, my walk, my features, my very being. By the time we passed, I would be consumed with embarrassment … why? Heaven knows.

And it was happening again.

Woman on bench, older, well built, probably, under the loose coat. Straggly grey hair hung shoulder length. She watched me, expressionless. And as I passed, raised the can of lager to her mouth.

Going somewhere I suppose. Home? Or going to work?

Nice taking weight off me feet. No rush. Nowhere to go and nothing to do. Nice here, bit warmer than yesterday. It might do. No worse than some places and darn sight better than some. And have I seen some! Not that it mattered; then or now, didn't matter, nothing did. Still doesn't except … except I've stopped fighting, it's never got me anywhere.

Now I'll just settle for peace and quiet. Watch the world go by. Someone said that once, wonder who. And why? Had he - or was it she – given up and settled for some peace and quiet? Like me.

Like her what's just gone by. Looked like she enjoys a bit of peace and quiet. None of that searching, fighting. Just content with her lot. Well, I'm having a bit of that now. Might get to like it. Just drop this can in the bin, get meself a six pack and just mosey along home. Yup, might as well call it home, think I'm staying.

Sad, that's what it is, I thought, reaching that age and sitting on a park bench, looking more than dishevelled and drinking a can of beer at that time in the morning. Once upon a time I'd have thought it disgusting but now I think it's sad, sad to look so lost and aimless and alone. Wonder what happens to such people – something must happen. She can't have spent her whole life like that. Perhaps she was married, and he's left her, gone off with someone else – bit of totty from the office as they say. Or he's died, suddenly she's a widow and not coping with the loneliness very well.

338

Perhaps she's not the victim, perhaps she left him! Had a bit of an affair and went off … riding into the sunset and all that … But it's not worked out. Wonder if she regrets it?

Lady with Lager faded from my mind as I opened the front door to hear the washing machine on final spin. Just in time to hang things on the line and enjoy the feeling of a job well done – albeit by a machine, my only input being loading and pressing the button. Still feel as though I rank with the woman baking her bread in a firepit as she crossed the prairie in a covered wagon as I peg garments on the line.

Laundry mentally ticked, I skip over Weed flower beds and start making a Shopping list – this proves irksome as I know I should phone and confirm numbers first. No point in shopping if they can't all come. Abandon shopping list, pick up phone and WhatsApp everyone. Continue with shopping list, can just adjust quantities once I know how many.

An image of Lager Lady floats into my mind, wonder if she has friends to share meals with. Wonder if she's deserted wife, widow, rejected mistress, failed entrepreneur … or what.

This walking every day has become such a habit. All thanks to Bernard! Will try to feel as positive once winter comes; in the meantime, lovely way to start the day.

She's back. Lager Lady. Can see her on the bench in the distance. I did wonder what happened ... where did she go ... was she ill? Thought she might have moved away. She was there most mornings, just sitting, can in hand usually. And sometimes smoking. Wondered if she is a bag lady but she never has more than a can, or two. In town they seem to stash their sleeping bags and rucksack in certain doorways. I used to think how trusting but then realised they know only too well no one would be interested in their worldly belongings. Or them. Wish she wouldn't just sit there, watching. Used to wonder if she actually sees me? Or is she just gazing vacantly into space?

But then one morning, unnerved or perhaps sorry for her ... I said 'Morning' and was rewarded with a 'Morning' back. Once started of course, social niceties had to be observed and every morning we would exchange a 'Morning'. Once or twice a 'Good morning'. Interesting how the three syllables require so much more effort than the two syllable Bon jour – and the latter flows more easily from the mouth which has to articulate quite separately the good-morn-ing.

Once or twice, I wondered if we would progress to a 'Nice weather' or some such. I felt it would have to be me. Felt she was waiting for me to make the first move. And then what? How and to what would it all progress? So, as I passed 'Morning' and again a 'Morning' in return. Did I detect a faint hint of a smile as she lifted her can? I still wondered where she was, where she went, was she ill, perhaps she has family after all.

Good to be back. Like old times. Me back on me bench in the park and her passing. Back in the old routine.

Can't say I didn't enjoy it. At first. Seemed a nice bloke, Tommy. We got on well together at first. Made me smile with his comments on people going by. We used to meet up at the Crown and have a few drinks. Would walk down to the river together, sit and watch the seagulls.

And when he said his sister had said he could use her caravan over at Watchet, I thought it would make a nice change. And he paid the bus fares, said it was his treat. It was all right at first. We would get up late - which took a bit of getting used to – get a few beers then sit down by the beach and watch the seagulls, watch the world go by.

It was after the first week things changed. I was enjoying the novelty,

341

hadn't seen the sea for a long time. But he started talking about me moving in with him permanent like. Kept talking about how we'd be better off sharing costs. Said he missed a bit of home cooking. Thought I could see where he was heading. It was when he said, being a bit younger, if I fancied a part time job he wouldn't stand in my way! Ha! Must have thought I was born yesterday.

Nah. Wasn't having any of that. Didn't say much, just nodded as if I was taking note, thinking it over. Well, thought it over all right. And made up me mind. But thought I'd best keep quiet, make the most of the time by the sea. That was grand. Watching the waves splashing in, the gulls floating on air currents and all the folks walking by.

All I wanted was for him to offer to pay the fares back. Which he did. And then I broke it to him. Nothing doing, said I appreciated the offer, but it just weren't for me. Think he was disappointed, said he was, but know I'm better on me own. Better off with me own thoughts and might have beens.

And if I go off on one there's only me to worry about.

Here she comes again. Little Miss Busy. Always walks as if she's going somewhere, got something to do.

'Morning'.

Funny.

I'm sort of glad she's back. At least I know she is OK. Not dead in a doorway somewhere. But what a life. Sitting on a bench in a park with a can of beer. Wonder what else she does for the rest of the day. Does she live near?

Part of me thinks I should offer a bit more of a greeting. And then think where would it lead – would she become one of those garrulous sorts who needs to talk endlessly but to no end? Do I want to get involved? Would she want to tell me … things?

I saw her one morning, it had been raining so the bench looked still wet and she was sitting there, can in one hand, cigarette in the other. The sky was still overcast, could well rain again. Felt a bit concerned, wondered how long she had been sitting there, was her coat wet? Suppose she'd said she had nowhere to go, would I have felt obliged to offer her sanctuary? And where would all that lead?

So I walked on.

She was there again next day, sitting with sunlight on her face as she smiled and nodded.

'Morning' we said.

And I was glad she was OK.

Love the colours of Autumn … the reds and oranges and purples and the way the leaves rustle under my feet. Wonder what the squirrels find to eat here? Sycamores mostly, but I guess there are enough acorns and hazel nuts from the wood alongside the park. So why don't they stay in the wood? Why are there always squirrels here in the park scurrying up the trunks and along the branches?

Lager Lady has a friend! He was sitting on her other side, almost obscured by her trailing raincoat as I approached. A thin little man, also clutching a can. She was gazing into the distance, glanced as I neared and I could almost swear she had a hint of a smile, almost as if she were pleased to see me.

'Morning' we said.

And she smiled. So I did. And passed.

Had the impression they knew each other. Friends? Passing acquaintances? Why should I care? Not that I do, but just thought he looked small and weaselly and she was worth more than that. She might look scruffy … unkempt … but he looked seedy, unwashed.

Was surprised to see Tommy. In the park. See him at the Crown upon occasion, we have a drink together, pass the time of day. But took me by surprise, turning up in the park. Said he'd come to ask if I'd change me mind. But this lady's not for turning (someone said that once, can't remember where) so we just talked a bit. He kept saying he could tell I was lonely, that I could do with a bit of company, and so could he.

And along comes Miss Busy. On her regular constitutional, saw her coming way off. Walks as if she has somewhere to go, wonder if she lives near the park.

'Morning' we said as she passed, and she gave a big smile.

Of course, Tommy wanted to know who she was, and I said, ' Oh just one of me friends'. He looked a bit surprised, suppose he hadn't expected me to have any friends. Looked a bit put out. He didn't stay long after that, said he'd see me around and I said yes. Said I'd see him at the Crown. Didn't really want him here with me, next thing is he might expect me to ask him home for a drink.

First signs of winter, hard frost in the night. Opened

the curtains and looked out at the sharply defined configurations of my transformed garden, shivered and told myself firmly that it would be very bracing once I got going.

It's the getting going! I took my time.

And it was actually very pleasant indeed; the sun was not warm but the air sparkled and everywhere had that fresh new look. Walking every day meant I have built up a comfortable rhythm and I can walk along quite briskly feeling that glow of self-righteousness when involved in Daily Exercise.

Despite the frost it was not that cold, already the temperature had risen and in places the crisp whiteness was fading. Leaves which had been hesitating, had fallen in drifts of browns and oranges, many still with frosted edges. Two squirrels raced each other, leaping from tree to tree.

To my surprise, Lager Lady was already seated on her bench. Surely she hadn't been there all night? was my first thought. She looked warm enough in her woolly hat pulled firmly down over her ears and a bright red scarf encircled her neck several times. She nodded and smiled as I approached.

'Morning,' we said.

'Bit chilly,' I added.

'Yes, it is,' she said.

Bit chilly? Bloody cold first thing but thought I'd make the effort. Nice to talk to someone early in the day.

THE FRIDGE WAS EMPTY

The cock crowed again, having greeted the dawn a couple of hours earlier he could now turn his attention to his scrawny wives.

Musonda yawned, stretched. And slowly heaved herself up from the bed. She wrapped a length of citenge round her waist and picked up the blanket. Walking outside she shook it vigorously before stretching it over a nearby bush. And then the second blanket joined its fellow. Back inside the hut she turned the thin mattress over, the rough pole framework of the bed didn't make itself too painfully felt if she observed that daily ritual.

The early morning sun was bright but not yet hot as she squinted down the patch of beaten, well-swept earth to where the hens were leisurely scratching and occasionally pecking at some, to her, unseen seed or insect. The cock, perched on an upturned crate, stretched his neck and crowed again – his head turned to the heavens but his eyes on his harem below.

Slowly Musonda poured some water from the bottle into the enamel bowl and after screwing the cap back on, proceeded to wash her hands and face.

And then placed a few thin twigs, dry grass and dry leaves into last night's ashes and lit a precious match as she gently shook some more dry grass over the hesitant flame. And squatting down, blew long and slow. The flames flickered more strongly so she could then place a few small logs over the fire and pour some water from the large plastic bottle into her pan. Balancing it over the three fire stones, she left it to heat while she swept the hut floor with her bound bunch of long thin twigs.

She swept under the bed and across the floor and then swept all the dust and few leaves out onto the yard and across towards the bananas. She took her time, there was no need for haste. Throwing a handful of crushed maize kernels for the hens, she watched as they pecked furiously at the largesse. The water was bubbling – time to pour some precious hot water on to a few tea leaves in the enamel mug. As it steamed in the thin air, she took last night's cold nsima from a bowl and chewed it thoughtfully, taking slow tentative sips of the steaming tea.

The water bottle was still half full - enough until the

afternoon when she would walk down to the tap. Long ago she had been used to walking down to the river with her friends, cheerfully chatting and laughing as they carried their empty pots and – for the more prosperous – enamel pails bought from the Indian store. There they had a leisurely filling as they cooled their feet at the water's edge, always aware to watch for drifting eyes of an opportunist crocodile. Walking back, heavy containers balanced on heads on a rolled strip of old citenge, had been slower under the hot sun.

Since the charity Water Aid had installed a borehole with pump and tap at the end of the village, the walk for water was shorter and she would make it alone. A few of her age group were left and, like her, had survived tired years raising grandchildren orphaned in the Aids epidemic.

For a time, as the grandchildren grew, they had fetched and carried water but now most of them were gone. Gone to far off towns, in search of jobs, sending money back at intervals. Money which was useful at the Indian store a few miles away up on the main road to town. They would walk there, Musonda and a few friends, when a new pail or bowl was needed. Once there they would leisurely examine the goods on shelves and in piles on the floor. Examine, compare, puzzle over a new item,

351

shake their heads over prices. The storekeeper ignored them, concentrating on his cell phone. The assistants too, knew to wait. A sale was sure – there was nowhere else to go. Eventually, choices made, there might be an extra purchase after much head shaking and soft 'Aa-a's', a length of bright new citenge, a pair of plastic flip flops, a bar of soap, packet of salt, candles …

And then the long walk back, purchases carefully bundled and carried on heads while a hand switched flies away with a plucked leaf spray. Gossip was as much of long ago as of items seen but not bought. There were no infants now on their backs – there were few children in the village in fact. Sometimes they were brought from town on brief visits – but had to return for the all-important schooling without which there was no future in towns. For who would want to return to the village? it was fine to keep in touch with their roots, yet electric lights and shops crammed with desirable but expensive goods always beckoned.

Musonda was able to tend her few crops and chickens and barter with others. Like her peers, she was living much as her parents and grandparents had – hand to mouth subsistence farming. That brief spell of developing Government health care and education had waned and fractured as Aids swept the country and the survivors had learned to adapt or maintain the old ways.

Musonda was more fortunate than some. Her four children had lived and had basic education, walking to the primary school only five miles away. She and her husband had worked hard to make sure their children completed the seven years to grade 7 and all four had progressed to Town, finding jobs, sending money home. And then Aids. Only her son Aaron had survived. He alone now sent her money. Not that she had great need now that the seven grandchildren she had cared for had gone. Aaron had brought them home to the village after each sibling succumbed to Aids.They in turn had eventually left for Town.

Musonda had never been to Town. Had listened – as had most of her generation – to the tales of wonderful ways that the town people lived. Electric lights and cars. Electric cookers and shops, larger than they could imagine. Houses that had houses built on top – The only way she could visualise multi storey buildings. So much sounded desirable and yet, they had noticed that, on the rare visits, their fortunate relations from Town would sigh with contentment, sit quietly round fires under the stars, rolling relish into the ball of nsima in their palms and eat with enjoyment.

They seemed to envy the village life – but would not stay – must get back to Meetings and Business and that strange Town life. They came less often now that the grandchildren had joined their elders and were preoccupied with jobs.

Musonda would walk to the post office at Mwense ten miles away from time to time. Check if there were any post and walk home again. Occasionally there would be a message, relayed from person to person 'Tell Musonda in Shi Mukanje's village there is mail'.

Her first born, Aaron, never forgot. And, long ago, he had visited. Had arrived with a friend - they were 'in Business' together. They were making money, good money and were able to employ some relatives. And he had brought her a bonsela - a gift. Admittedly a trifle premature. But he and his friend were sure, they knew for certain, Progress and Development were the key words. The Government had promised. With independence a brighter richer future for all beckoned.

And Musonda was proud of her gift, even though she did not quite understand it. Aaron had said, his friend nodding wisely, that he would share his good fortune with his mother. Not like some who forgot their roots and relations back in the village. Her first born was different.

He had made sure that her hut had a corrugated tin roof, transporting the shiny sheets himself and paying neighbours to reroof her hut with a tin roof which would last for ever! And he had not criticised her on his next visit, agreeing that the thatch over the tin roof did keep it cooler.

His last gift – so long since she had seen him – stood in the corner waiting for the long-promised Government electricity. She did not understand how this big box could always be cold inside. But Aaron had said it would be so. So, then it would be so.

But for now, she dusted this shining white box – this Wafridgie – and occasionally opened the door to admire the shelves waiting to cool her water. One day.

THE TREE

August 1978

Back then I lived in Zambia, just outside the capital Lusaka.

We had built a house on Leopards Hill Road about ten miles from the town boundary, where the city ended in a straight line at Lake Road. At Lake Road the town ended, bush began.

Driving home, work, shopping, visiting, whatever, behind me, I would be alone on a dirt road, bordered on both sides with grass and an occasional scrubby small tree for as far as the eye could see. The grass grew lush and green, six feet tall in the rainy season but gradually faded over the months of the dry season to orange and then to bleached pale, pale yellow by the October sun. The grass rippled like waves in the sea, was swayed by the winds. Overhead an endless expanse of sky, stretching from horizon to horizon, drained blue white in heat, piercing blue, purple with storm clouds – I might feel

357

like an intrepid explorer, alone in my quest or a voyager, alone and at peace.

Always, I welcomed the ten miles driving home, alone across the grassy sea. And on my right, after a few miles, there was a tree.

And what a tree it must have been. Had it once been one of these small scrubby thorny little things? Hard to imagine it.

My special tree, the one I looked for, about half a mile from the roadside, had been huge; my eyes were drawn to it until it was left behind. It must have been enormous, a giant of a tree. I would wonder what animals had sheltered underneath from the midday sun or stormy downpours, had lived in its branches which must have spread wide and far. It would have been tall, perhaps a landmark for travellers before this road was made.

I liked to think of an elephant, its trunk reaching up to pull down a leafy spray, to stuff in its wide mouth. Had giraffe ambled past, pausing to nibble at some high morsel? Surely a troop of baboons, had taken refuge from some predator in its sturdy branches. Perhaps a pride of lions had slept off some kill in its shade, perhaps had watched the arrival of the railway in the far, far distance, heard the chugging of the first steam engines and known it was time to retreat.

And now, it was still a landmark, albeit a reduced one. But nevertheless, a tree to search for, keep in sight and, as I did, admire and appreciate each time I passed. Had it suffered in a bush fire? Succumbed to some disease? Or merely, ancient, died back, bit by bit, branch by branch until only the main trunk was left? Bark long gone, the wood honed smooth by wind and rain, bleached and scorched by October suns, tree now stood stout, proud, erect, alone. Naked on the savannah, tree stood there still; one could see where three strong branches had begun, had reached out to embrace life. Jagged edges marked their beginnings, marked their end.

Had the fallen branches flamed and turned to ashy embers in some fire.? Or had wandering women, seized upon the fallen wood, breaking it into manageable lengths to tie into bundles, to carry home on their heads, as they gossiped along a beaten track?

I wished each time I passed, that tree stood on my land. That I could walk to it each day, lay my hand on its smooth side, perhaps I would lean against it, listening to its heartbeat. For somehow, I believed, tree would know I was there, that someone cared.

The day that I left, tears pricked my eyes as, passing, I said goodbye.

February 2020

I went back. I had said I never would, but the pull was too strong.

I went back, knowing it could not be the same. Commonsense said nothing stays the same forever. Friends told me I would be amazed, astounded at the changes. Lusaka had become a sprawling city, sporting tarmac dual carriageways, tall buildings reared up across the skyline, shopping malls offered all that the heart could desire.

I knew. I understood. But could not imagine.

Still saw the ways and areas in my mind, believed I would recognise the old places, find them amongst the new.

Of course, it was not to be.

Even the airport was swallowed up in the maelstrom of development, was no longer a landmark set apart in the vast expanse of savannah. Driven here and there by welcoming friends, I dutifully admired this new building,

360

that sweeping new road, the new shopping malls (there had been none before). And here and there, just occasionally, I would spot some long-lost friend, a small building, shy and retiring among its new neighbours. Perhaps a junction seemed familiar for a moment, before the eye succumbed to changes. And everywhere, the billboards. Billboards such as I had never imagined. Flanking the roads, the dual carriageways, in endless succession, enormous billboards exhorting one to buy, to see, to enjoy, to eat, to drink…

It was a battering of the senses.

After a few days, we were to drive along Leopards Hill Road to visit friends who lived past my former home. My whole body relaxed as we set off, this would be a gentle drive filled with memories – and I would see my tree. He would be unchanged.

'You know where we are now?' the query broke my reverie.

Gazing at the solid lines of traffic on all sides, I admitted I had no idea.

'Lake Road! Remember, where we join Leopards Hill Road – your road, remember?'

How could I?

Heavy traffic, crawling nose to tail, two large shopping malls near a half-constructed flyover, more shops, stalls, displays of huge concrete garden pots confronted me on all sides. We joined the slow queue of traffic on to Leopards Hill Road as I gazed about me in bewilderment.

Where was the grass? The space? The air? For God's sake, where was the sky?

Found the sky of course, peering up and sideways.

But rippling waves of grassy sea were no more.

And tree. I could not, would not, imagine his end.

Printed in Great Britain
by Amazon

29098341R00207